"Do something," Jake cried. "Anything!"

The Cardassian launched another volley of his plasma weapons.

The engines of the *Ganges* stuttered to life, and the ship nudged forward . . . then the power died again. Cardassian plasma bolts came in at full power. Jake and Nog had no shields, no mobility. There was no escape.

"Hang on," Jake cried as a sound like exploding thunder rammed into the back of the runabout.

"We're hit!" Nog said, screaming over the din.

A second, stronger bolt crashed into them, and Jake had only an instant to spin around in his pilot's chair before the back bulkhead of the *Ganges* erupted in blue-hot flames.

The engine exploded, igniting the antimatter core. The entire runabout disintegrated into an expanding tidal wave of glowing energy that surrounded Jake with a brilliant glare that gradually faded. . . .

—leaving only the terrible, bright green words hanging in the air of the Arcade holosuite:

GAME OVER.

But the real *game had not even begun . . .*

Star Trek: The Next Generation
STARFLEET ACADEMY

Star Trek: Deep Space Nine

Star Trek movie tie-in

Star Trek Generations

STAR TREK
DEEP SPACE NINE®

HIGHEST SCORE

KEM ANTILLES

Interior illustrations by
Todd Cameron Hamilton

A MINSTREL® BOOK

PUBLISHED BY POCKET BOOKS

New York   London   Toronto   Sydney   Tokyo   Singapore

A MINSTREL PAPERBACK *Original*

 A Minstrel Book published by
POCKET BOOKS, a division of Simon & Schuster Inc.
1230 Avenue of the Americas, New York, NY 10020

A VIACOM COMPANY

ISBN: 0-671-89936-8

First Minstrel Books printing June 1996

10 9 8 7 6 5 4 3 2 1

Cover art by Alan Gutierrez

Printed in the U.S.A.

A million thanks to Lillie E. Mitchell for her typing; Richard Curtis for his agenting skills, and Lisa Clancy for her editing skills; and my friends Kevin J. Anderson, Rebecca Moesta, Mark Budz, Marina Fitch, and Michael Paul Meltzer, without whom this book could never have been written

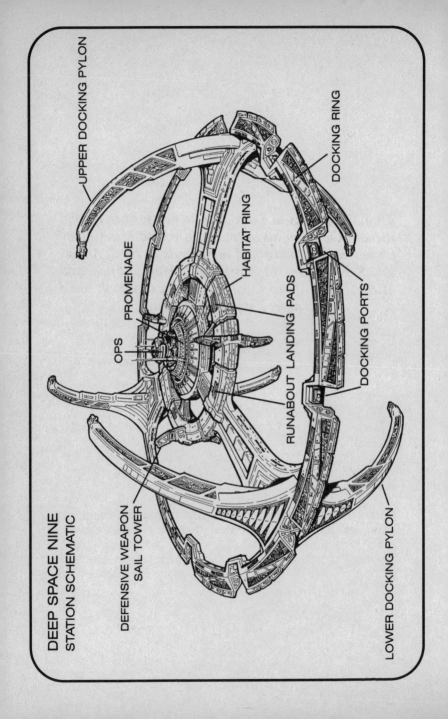

DEEP SPACE NINE
STATION SCHEMATIC

UPPER DOCKING PYLON

DOCKING RING

HABITAT RING

PROMENADE

OPS

RUNABOUT LANDING PADS

DOCKING PORTS

DEFENSIVE WEAPON
SAIL TOWER

LOWER DOCKING PYLON

STAR TREK®: DEEP SPACE NINE™
Cast of Characters

JAKE SISKO—Jake is a young teenager and the only human boy permanently on board Deep Space Nine. Jake's mother died when he was very young. He came to the space station with his father but found very few kids his own age. He doesn't remember life on Earth, but he loves baseball and candy bars, and he hates homework. His father doesn't approve of his friendship with Nog.

NOG—He is a Ferengi boy whose primary goal in life—like all Ferengi—is to make money. His father, Rom, is frequently away on business, which is fine with Nog. His uncle, Quark, keeps an eye on him. Nog thinks humans are odd with their notions of trust and favors and friendship. He doesn't always understand Jake, but since his father forbids him to hang out with the human boy, Nog and Jake are best friends. Nog loves to play tricks on people, but he tries to avoid Odo whenever possible.

COMMANDER BENJAMIN SISKO—Jake's father has been appointed by Starfleet Command to oversee the operations of the space station and act as a liaison between the Federation and Bajor. His wife was killed in a Borg attack, and he is raising Jake by himself. He is a very busy man who always tries to make time for his son.

ODO—The security officer was found by Bajoran scientists years ago, but Odo has no idea where he originally came from. He is a shape-shifter, and thus can assume any shape for a period of time. He normally maintains a vaguely human appearance but every sixteen hours he must revert to his natural liquid state. He has no patience for lawbreakers and less for Ferengi.

MAJOR KIRA NERYS—Kira was a freedom fighter in the Bajoran underground during the Cardassian occupation of Bajor. She now represents Bajoran interests aboard the station and is Sisko's first officer. Her temper is legendary.

LIEUTENANT JADZIA DAX—An old friend of Commander Sisko's, the science officer Dax is actually two joined entities known as the Trill. There a separate consciousness—a symbiont—in the young female host's body. Sisko knew the symbiont Dax in a previous host, which was a "he."

DR. JULIAN BASHIR—Eager for adventure, Doctor Bashir graduated at the top of his class and requested a deep-space posting. His enthusiasm sometimes gets him into trouble.

MILES O'BRIEN—Formerly the Transporter Chief aboard the *U.S.S. Enterprise,* O'Brien is now Chief of Operations on Deep Space Nine.

KEIKO O'BRIEN—Keiko was a botanist on the *Enterprise,* but she moved to the station with her husband and her young daughter, Molly. Since there is little use for her botany skills on the station, she is the teacher for all of the permanent and traveling students.

QUARK—Nog's uncle and a Ferengi businessman by trade, Quark runs his own combination restaurant/casino/holosuite venue on the Promenade, the central meeting place for much of the activity on the station. Quark has his hand in every deal on board and usually manages to stay just one step ahead of the law—usually in the shape of Odo.

CHAPTER 1

As the runabout *Mekong* shot through the Wormhole at top speed, young Jake Sisko fought with the controls of the small craft.

"Hang on!" Jake called to his Ferengi friend Nog, who sat in the copilot's seat. "It's going to be a bumpy ride."

The bald-headed Ferengi boy tugged on his huge, scrolled ears and squinted at the tactical station. "I'm prepared for anything," he said in his raspy voice. His blue-nailed fingers danced over the buttons, prepping the weapons-system controls. "We've got to get back to Deep Space Nine before the ceremony starts, or we'll be in big trouble!"

In front of them, the swirling, flashing colors of the Wormhole opened up like a giant round doorway into black space. The *Mekong* streaked through, heading back toward home.

"Look out!" Nog cried.

Directly across their bow, a cloud of cratered rubble

appeared, suddenly springing into crystal focus. Jagged lumps of rock flew through space, crisscrossing their path, ready to destroy anything that crashed into them.

"A meteor storm! Use the phasers, Nog," Jake shouted. "I'm taking evasive action."

"Our shields are almost at zero from that last Orion attack," Nog said. "We can't take much more."

The runabout plunged into the swarm of deadly meteoroids, dodging and spinning. Jake switched the command controls to manual and rolled the spacecraft between two tumbling boulders, each the size of a cargo transport. Jake could see the pockmarked, stony surface below him as the runabout scraped by. "That was close!"

Nog punched the weapons controls. "Targeting phasers now," he said.

An icy meteoroid hurtled in front of them, directly on a collision course. Nog fired twice. The red-orange explosions from the phasers cracked the rock. A third blast turned the meteoroid into a cloud of glowing space rubble.

"Good shot!" Jake said, laughing.

The runabout crashed through the debris cloud with scattered thumps and clangs as the rock fragments battered the smooth white hull of the ship.

"Give me a damage report," Jake called.

Nog punched up one of the tactical screens and scanned a diagram of the *Mekong*. "Could have been a lot worse. But our shields are failing—and we've got to make it back to DS9, or else!"

"How much time do we have?" Jake asked.

"Only about one standard hour," Nog answered after checking the chronometer. "If we don't use the talisman to stop the ceremony, that bomb is going to blow up the whole station!"

"We'll make it," Jake said in a low voice, gritting his teeth. "We have to." He didn't let himself relax for a moment as he punched the impulse engines, adding a burst of acceleration. He looked out the right cockpit window just in time to see another broken meteoroid streaking toward them.

"To the side!" Nog cried.

With their shields weakened, Jake's only defense was to dodge. He rammed the engines to maximum speed, and the runabout jerked forward. Jake and Nog both cried out as the immediate acceleration shoved them against their piloting seats, but the meteoroid came on—too big and too fast.

The *Mekong* almost escaped . . . but the careening rock clipped the port engine pod, sending the ship spinning out of control. The stars cycled around them like a whirlpool of white streaks outside the front ports.

"Stabilize, stabilize!" Jake cried.

Nog, his small eyes wide open in terror, pounded the control board. "I'm trying," he said. He hit more buttons. "Major damage to the starboard warp nacelle."

The runabout wheeled out of control, and the scattered stars in the sky made Jake feel dizzy. His stomach tightened as he used every ounce of his piloting knowledge, firing short bursts from the impulse engines to stop

4

the runabout's dizzying plunge through the meteor storm.

"Doesn't look good," Jake said, flashing a sidelong glance to Nog at the tactical station. "We're crippled. It's going to take all of our skill just to crawl back to Deep Space Nine. And that bomb is still ticking."

The Ferengi boy took another glance at his tactical screens and froze. "Uh-oh," Nog said. "Look who's coming out of the Wormhole!"

The Wormhole flared, dilating and spilling out one of the deadly Orion ships.

"I guess we didn't get away from him after all," Jake said.

"I'll bet he's mad at us," Nog observed.

"We've got to squeeze all the speed we can out of these engines. If we get close enough to Deep Space Nine," Jake said, "they'll turn on their shields and protect us."

"Unless the station blows up first," Nog said, his voice tinged with panic. "How are we going to move with only one engine?" Nog checked his screens again. "The Orion is powering up his weapons! We're doomed!"

Jake slammed the impulse engine controls past the red-line maximums. The *Mekong* responded sluggishly, but he did not dare let up, trying to maneuver around the flying debris at the edge of the meteor cloud. "The Orion's got to come through this meteor shower just like we do, right?"

"But his shields are at full strength—unlike ours!" Nog said. "If you hit one of those rocks, we're done for."

"And if we let that Orion catch us," Jake said, "we're

just as done for. He wants to destroy that talisman at all costs."

"Surrender and prepare to be boarded," came the threatening voice of the Orion commander. "You are doomed."

"Should we call for help?" Nog said. "Maybe your father could—"

"No!" Jake shouted. "We can do this ourselves."

The Orion fired a plasma burst from his ship, but the bolt went wide, striking one of the nearby meteoroids.

"Too close," Nog said. The patter and thump of blasted meteoroid chunks struck them again. "More hull damage, a couple of microleaks," Nog continued. "Our shields are completely gone."

The ship swooped down on them, powering up its weapons systems again. A second plasma burst sizzled past, burning so close that Jake imagined he could feel the ionization crackle through the hull of the *Mekong*.

"We should surrender," Nog said. "We don't have a chance."

"What's the point in surrendering?" Jake said. His voice grew high-pitched with tension. "Don't give up on me now, Nog. The whole station is at stake if we don't get out of this."

The Ferengi boy took a deep breath and nodded.

"Look, I've got an idea," Jake said, punching down on the controls. "See that fringe of the meteor cloud? We'll go toward that, hide and seek. It's our last chance for cover."

Nog looked out the front port windows, seeing the

forest of space rocks. "You're going *toward* the meteors?"

"Yes," Jake said, drumming his fingers on the control panel. "I'm going to jettison our damaged nacelle and detonate it. Maybe the Orion will think we crashed into one of the meteoroids and blew up. As soon as the nacelle detonates, I want a full shutdown. Turn everything off. We'll hang dead in space." He swallowed nervously. "There's a chance he won't notice us."

"But there's a chance he will," Nog said.

"I didn't say it was a very *good* chance. Besides, we don't have any better choice," Jake answered. He changed course, arrowing toward the scattered rocks.

The Orion ship increased speed to pursue, weapons systems glowing and ready to fire. Jake knew the ship wouldn't miss a third shot.

When the last of the meteoroids swept past them, Jake dodged as best he could with the sluggish controls. As soon as several of the rocks came between him and the other ship, Jake jettisoned the smoldering warp nacelle from the bottom of the runabout. The *Mekong* spun out of control.

Jake shielded his eyes as he saw the cylindrical engine pod tumbling in a sparking arc toward the meteoroid.

"Three . . . two . . . one," he counted—and just as the Orion crossed over the fringe of the largest meteoroid, the warp nacelle blew up, showering space with flying shards of metal and glowing debris.

"Full shutdown, while his sensors are blinded!" Jake cried. Together, he and the Ferengi boy frantically switched off their running lights, shut down their impulse engines, and removed all trace of their energy signature in space.

"Now, we wait," Jake said, sitting in the darkness. The cockpit of the runabout was lit only by the starlight. In the distance, he could see the glittering lights of Deep Space Nine, impossibly far away. Meanwhile, the hidden doomsday bomb on the station continued its countdown, and only Jake and Nog had the power to stop it—but first they had to escape.

"We're like sitting waterfowl," Nog said.

"Not if we manage to fool him," Jake said, keeping his fingers crossed.

But, as they watched, the Orion continued on course, straight toward them. The firing ports of his plasma weapons glowed, ready to fire.

"No good!" Nog said.

"Get those engines on again!" Jake shouted. "We have to make a run for it."

"I can't start the engines cold," Nog said. "They won't work."

"Well, do something," Jake yelled. "Anything!"

The Orion fired his plasma weapons. The engines of the *Mekong* stuttered to life, and the ship nudged forward . . . then the power died again. Orion plasma bolts came in at full power. Jake and Nog had no shields, no mobility.

There was no escape.

"Hang on," Jake cried as a sound like exploding thunder rammed into the back of the runabout.

"We're hit, Jake!" Nog screamed over the din.

A second, stronger bolt crashed into them, and Jake had only an instant to spin around in his pilot's chair before the back bulkhead of the *Mekong* erupted in blue-hot flames.

The engine exploded, igniting the antimatter core. The entire runabout disintegrated into an expanding tidal wave of glowing energy that surrounded Jake with a brilliant glare . . .

. . . leaving only the terrible, bright green words hanging in the air of the Arcade game booth:

GAME OVER.

Nog's eyes glittered with excitement as he gave up the simulator controls and stood rubbing his clawed hands together. "Did you see that, Jake? Look at our score. That's the highest we've ever gotten!"

Jake still felt disoriented from the sudden end of the game. He looked around the blank simulator room until he saw the numerical value of the score they had achieved. It cheered him up to see how well they had done—but not well enough.

"I still wish we could get all the way to the end of the game just once."

"Jake, nobody's ever made it all the way through this simulation, not even professional pilots."

Jake nodded. "Yeah, but nobody's practiced as much as we have, either. We've spent every free hour at this game for the last month."

"Next time," Nog said with a grin. He looked at his wrist chronometer in sudden alarm. "I need to get back to Quark's!" he said. "My uncle told me I have to work this afternoon. If I'm late, he'll be very angry."

As the Ferengi boy scuttled toward the door of the Arcade, Jake followed him. "See you here tomorrow?" Jake said.

"Okay. Let's try to do better," Nog answered, then dashed out into the Promenade toward his uncle's bar and casino.

Back in their quarters, Jake's father, Commander Benjamin Sisko, was not so pleased to hear about his son's highest score.

"Jake," Commander Sisko said, "don't you think you've been spending altogether too much time in the Arcade? I can tell you're getting very good at it, and I'm proud for your sake, but what good is all that practice going to do you? It won't benefit you later in life."

Jake shrugged in exasperation. "Dad, I wasn't thinking about what *good* it would do me. Nog and I have fun, and besides," he said with a hopeful smile, "it keeps us out of trouble, doesn't it? You told us to find something that would keep us out of trouble."

Sisko's frown turned up with the slightest hint of a smile. "I'd rather you put a little variety into your free time. Something that could help you in your future career."

Jake sighed. "There's nothing else to do on this station." He sat down on his bed and folded his hands in his lap as he stared at the floor plates.

"How about studying?" Sisko said.

"Oh, Dad!" Jake said.

"Look, Jake," Sisko said, "I don't want to be hard on you, because I know you didn't want to come to Deep Space Nine in the first place. But don't you think you're getting old enough that you should start considering what you want to do with your life? I know you don't necessarily want to go into Starfleet, but you should at least start considering something, some goal to work toward. Why not concentrate on your writing?"

"I will, Dad. Don't worry."

"All right, enough lecturing," Sisko said. "But do me a favor," he added. "From now on, let's limit your time in that Arcade to one hour a day, all right?"

Jake brightened. He had expected something far worse. "Okay, Dad. It's a deal."

Nog's uncle Quark was not quite so understanding.

"Where have you been, boy?" Quark said. "Go clean off those tables. New customers can't sit at a dirty table." Quark's Ferengi eyes flashed as he leaned over the young boy, who looked away in the standard gesture of respect. "And you know what it means when people can't sit at the tables? They can't buy drinks—and when they can't buy drinks, we don't make any latinum."

"Yes, Uncle," Nog said.

"That's an important rule of economics," Quark said. "Have you been at the Arcade again?"

Nog panicked, looked from side to side. "Uh, why do you ask, Uncle?"

Quark scowled. "I can smell it on you."

Nog grabbed an empty tray from behind the bar. Off at one of the Dabo tables, a crowd of players squealed in delight as they won. Quark whirled and clicked his sharp teeth together. "Bah! More losses for the house," he said.

"Uh, Uncle," Nog said, "I think I see some empty glasses over there and some dishes. I'll go clean them up right away."

Quark waggled a clawed finger at him. "You spend too much time at that Arcade, boy. You should be here working, earning a living."

"But I, uh"—Nog thought fast—"I'm doing research in entertainment systems." His words picked up speed as the excuse came to him. "Isn't that one of the Rules of Acquisition, to learn the customer's weaknesses so you can better take advantage of him?"

"Rule Number 87," Quark answered automatically.

Nog's father, Rom, scurried behind the bar and tripped, spilling a tray full of beverage containers. Quark whirled to snap at his brother. Luckily, most of the containers were empty, or Quark would have been much more upset.

As soon as Quark had finished yelling at him, Rom turned and glared at Nog. "And where have you been, my son?" he said. "We need your help here."

Quark brushed him away. "I'm taking care of this, Rom. You've got work to do. Get that table another selenium fizz—and don't go so heavy on the synthehol this time."

"Yes, Brother," Rom said, then scurried to the drink replicator station behind the bar.

"Now, you listen to me, boy," Quark said to Nog. "I think it's admirable that you're learning about entertainment systems. There could be a great career in it for you someday. But right now, you're working for me, here. Playing games in that Arcade is not going to help you out as much as putting in your time here."

"Yes, Uncle," Nog said. "From this point on, I will

limit my time there to . . ." He paused. "Two hours a day." Which was exactly the amount of time he currently spent.

"Ten minutes," Quark countered.

"One hour?" Nog asked hopefully.

"Agreed," Quark said. "Now, go clean those tables."

CHAPTER 2

The alien disembarked from a Bajoran transport shuttle, then stood alone.

As the other passengers came off the ship onto Deep Space Nine, they chattered with companions or looked around for points of contact. The alien, though, simply stopped, drinking in the details of the space station.

He had a narrow, birdlike face that tapered to a curving point of hardened skin around a long, toothless mouth slit. Nostril slashes rippled alongside the hardened beak, membranes flickering as the alien drew in the scents of Deep Space Nine. His skin was grayish brown, but a brilliant crest of glittering emerald-green scale feathers rippled from the base of his nose to a jeweled point on the top of his head. His eyes were solid black and glinted in the light of the station.

The alien had a purpose—and he knew exactly where he wanted to go.

As the other passengers jostled around him, he took

15

only a moment to gain his bearings. Then he set off for the Promenade and the Arcade.

Once there, he disregarded the swirling electronic noises of a thousand entertainment systems. Waving half a bar of gold-pressed latinum, he bribed one of the gaming attendants to allow him access into the computer scoring records of the most difficult simulations.

The curious attendant peered over the alien's shoulder, trying to spy the numbers that so interested the alien—but, with a shove of his horned fist, the alien knocked the attendant away.

"Privacy, please," he said. "I paid you enough."

The attendant frowned and then went off in search of other customers.

With a few commands expertly entered into the computer system, the alien managed to sort the numbers scrolling in front of him. His glittering black eyes narrowed.

Two players in particular stood out well above the other contestants. They consistently had the highest scores. Good reaction times. Good ingenuity. Excellent.

The alien's hard beak did not permit him a smile, but he nodded his head. The emerald-green crest trembled in the flickering light of the Arcade.

Jake Sisko and Nog. He would find them, and make them an offer they couldn't refuse.

The next day, Jake and Nog emerged from the sealed Arcade game booth, congratulating each other. Jake held up his hand in a high five, and Nog slapped it.

"We're partners," Nog said. "The best ever!"

Jake agreed with a laugh. "No one in the history of the station has ever successfully completed the 'Escape Through the Wormhole' simulation."

"Until now," Nog said, rubbing his clawed hands together. "We're the best."

"Do you think your uncle will get us something to celebrate—like an Antarian shake?" Jake asked hopefully.

Nog lowered his gaze. "We can ask," he said. Then his voice became quieter. "But I doubt it. There's no profit in celebrating."

They turned and glanced up to see a strange, tall alien step forward to block their way. He wore a padded tunic of some kind of dark green leather, polished to a bright glossiness. It reminded Jake of the shell of a scarab beetle.

"Excuse me," the alien said. His words had a warbling tone that made his voice sound musical and exotic. "You are the great gamers?" He indicated the glowing champions' score on the outer door of the Arcade, the highest score ever recorded there. "You are the skilled human Jake Sisko and the Ferengi Nog?"

"Yeah, that's us," Jake said.

"Allow me to congratulate you. My name is Kwiltek. Would you allow me to buy you something to commemorate your achievement?" he asked. "An Antarian shake for each of you, perhaps?"

Jake and Nog looked at each other, their eyes lighting up. "But what do you want?" Nog asked skeptically.

The alien's bobbing nod was like a bird pecking for insects. "I have a matter I wish to discuss with you . . . in more comfortable surroundings," Kwiltek trilled.

"Let's go to my uncle's place," Nog said, and they hurried off down the Promenade to Quark's.

Nog's father, Rom, was working behind the bar while Quark himself negotiated some sort of deal in the back room. The bar crowd was sparse in the mid-afternoon slow hours, and Rom eyed the boys suspiciously as they came in with the stranger and ordered two Antarian shakes.

"And how do you expect to pay for these luxuries?" Rom said, looking sidelong at Kwiltek. The birdlike alien reached a slender horned hand into his glossy green jerkin and withdrew several glittering pieces of metal.

"Ah, very well," Rom said, his face brightening. "Welcome to Quark's Place, sir." The older Ferengi flashed a look at his son. "You're welcome to bring friends like these in any time you like, boy. Can I get you anything, sir? Anything to drink?"

"Yes," Kwiltek answered. "I would like water. A glass of water."

Rom frowned. "Would you like anything in that?"

"Yes," Kwiltek answered. "I would like . . . ice."

Rom shuffled his feet, uncertain what to do. "There's a charge for that, you know. We don't give away free drinks."

"That is acceptable," Kwiltek answered.

Rom bustled away to get their orders as Jake and Nog followed the birdlike alien to a small table in the corner, far from other patrons.

Rom brought their drinks and then backed away, hesitating just within Ferengi earshot, and waited. He performed distracting duties as he clumsily tried to eavesdrop, but Kwiltek said nothing until Rom gave up in disgust and stomped back to the bar.

Kwiltek leaned closer to the boys and spoke quietly. "Allow me to explain myself," he said. "I am the administrator of an automated mining consortium. That probably sounds boring to great gamers like yourselves. But, trust me, your skills are exactly what I am looking for. I would like to offer you both a job—working for me."

"A job?" Nog sat up, grinning broadly and showing his sharp Ferengi teeth. "To earn real latinum?"

"Yes, real latinum," Kwiltek said.

Jake was more suspicious. He folded and unfolded his hands on the tabletop, then took a sip of his shake. "But what would you want us to do?" he said. "What skills do we have that a . . . a *mining company* could want?"

"Ah!" Kwiltek said, then made a fluting whistle. "Our mining company operates by *telepresence.* We send large excavating machines, ore haulers, and mineral extractors to hostile, uninhabitable planets. On these planets, fiery environments or terrible storms, earthquakes or poisonous atmospheres make it too dangerous to send in live workers."

He drew a musical breath through his nostril slits. He

stared down at them, his close-set eyes glittering. "So, instead, we park a mining station in orbit around one of these planets. Then we use simulators—very much like the ones in your Arcade game booths—with talented operators such as yourselves behind the controls, to direct the mining operations from long distance, in perfect safety. We get our ore. You get paid to play simulation games. And everyone is happy."

"Sounds good!" Nog said.

"What's the catch?" Jake asked. Already, he was wondering what his father would say.

"Ah," Kwiltek said with another fluting sound. "Because these mining operations are on very hazardous planets, we lose a good deal of machinery. That is why we need people with fast reaction speeds, with a genuine feel for how the machines work. We need good operators. Otherwise, we lose so much equipment through clumsy accidents that the value is barely offset by the precious minerals we mine.

"Of course, mining simulations can be rather dry and tedious, so we have embellished them—enhanced the telepresence machines so that you actually feel as if you are playing a game—by creating fake adversaries to fight." He spread his horned hands on the table next to Jake's. "We think you might enjoy it."

Jake listened to Kwiltek's words, but already possibilities rang through his mind. It would be fantastic to show his father that the skills he had developed by playing so many Arcade games had actually proven valuable, making him a prime candidate for an important job.

"We'll have to ask our parents," Jake said, "but there's a school vacation coming up soon. Maybe we could work during the break, on a trial basis?"

Kwiltek bobbed his head in a jerky nod again. "That would be acceptable," he said. "I will wait."

Commander Benjamin Sisko leaned across the bar, staring at Quark. Rom stood behind his brother, kneading his clawed hands together and letting Quark do the talking.

"So what do you think about all this, Quark?" Sisko said. "Does it sound too good to be true?"

"I think it's an intelligent business proposition," Quark answered quickly. "While it will be a great burden to lose the valuable assistance the boy has given me in the bar, Mr. Kwiltek has adequately compensated me for my inconvenience."

"And the pay is good, too," Rom interrupted.

"I believe it's the *boys'* pay," Sisko said.

"Yes, of course," Rom said. "We will place it in trust to be used for the betterment of the boy's later years."

"I see," Sisko said, not believing it for a minute. "I have to say that while I'm leery about letting Jake and Nog go off with this stranger, I have checked against Federation records and found that Kwiltek's mining company seems to be legitimate. They operate just the way he says, telepresent mining operations on uninhabitable worlds. They've just started operations in the Gamma Quadrant on the other side of the Wormhole."

Jake and Nog sat at one of the front tables, watching

the conversation. Jake's eyes were bright. "Please, Dad!" he said.

Sisko continued, "Jake and Nog do have the capabilities necessary for this particular job. Besides, I'm inclined to think it'll be a good credit for them in their employment files. It'll teach both boys some responsibility and give them job experience. And, provided we're allowed to keep in contact with them and receive regular progress reports"—he turned slowly to look at his son's beaming face—"I see no harm in letting them go off for a trial stint during the school break next week."

Jake and Nog jumped up and slapped each other's hands in congratulation.

"You're excited now," Sisko said, looking at them sternly, "but you may find that working a tough job isn't as fun as you think it'll be."

"Oh, Dad!" Jake said.

In the end, Quark did buy the boys an Antarian shake—a small one, to split—as a celebration gesture.

CHAPTER 3

I should be going, Uncle," Nog said anxiously. "I'd better not keep Kwiltek waiting."

"You don't meet him for another half hour," Quark said. "Plenty of time to finish setting up these tables for lunch. You're not trying to get out of finishing your work here, are you?"

Nog shook his head emphatically, hunching down. "No, Uncle! Of course not. How could you think such a thing?"

Quark flashed pointy teeth. "I thought not."

Nog's father, Rom, bustled up. "If he's late, Brother, I'm going to bill you for his lost pay."

Quark sneered. "Spending his latinum already, are you?"

Rom scowled, suddenly uncertain. "I am not! I just want to make sure the boy takes full advantage of this opportunity."

"So do I," Quark said. "Believe me, so do I. And the

sooner he gets these tables set up, the sooner he can start earning latinum for you."

Rom sputtered, then hurried off to attend to a table of rowdy Klingons clamoring for drinks.

Quark pulled Nog aside. "Listen, Nog, I want you to do me a little favor."

Nog eyed his uncle suspiciously. "What kind of favor?"

Quark leaned closer. "I want you find out everything you can about this mining operation and report back to me. What kind of ore they mine and how much. Who they're selling it to and at what price—that kind of thing. This could be a great business opportunity."

Nog crossed his thin arms over his chest. "Rule Number 29. What's in it for me?"

Quark rubbed his hands together. "A small pay raise when you get back."

"Hah! You want me to do your dirty work for that? Not good enough!"

Quark glanced over at Rom, who was bungling drink orders for the Klingons. "Shhh—not so loud! We don't want word about what you're doing to accidentally leak out, do we?" He turned back to the Ferengi boy. "Now, what sort of compensation did you have in mind for the simple little favor I asked?"

"Sixty percent of whatever profits you make from the information I provide," Nog said brashly. He felt his pulse racing with the excitement of the business deal. This was fun!

Quark made a choking sound. "Be reasonable!" he whispered.

"I am being reasonable. I'm doing all the work, and getting only a little more than half the profit."

Quark tilted his head, considering. "How about forty percent? Without me, the information you gather is useless. Knowing how to use that information is worth at least sixty percent."

Nog shook his head, blinking at his shrewd uncle. "Fifty-fifty," he said. "Otherwise, no deal."

Quark grimaced and slapped his forehead. "You'll ruin me! But . . . all right," he finally said. "Deal."

Nog couldn't keep from smiling. For once, he hadn't come out on the short end of a negotiation with his uncle.

"Come on." Jake heard Nog shout down the long corridor. "Kwiltek's waiting! The sooner we get started, the more credits we'll make." Jake's Ferengi friend raced across the shuttle bay to where the birdlike alien stood in the doorway of the mining company shuttle that had come to pick them up.

"Not so fast," Commander Sisko said, putting a firm hand on Jake's shoulder.

Jake paused, anxious to catch up with Nog, who was already boarding Kwiltek's ship. The last week of school had taken forever. Jake couldn't wait to see what Kwiltek had in store for them.

"But, Dad, I don't want to be late my first day at work," Jake said, turning to look at Sisko.

Sisko nodded. "Good. I'm glad to see you're treating this as a job, and not just another simulation game. Remember that, and you'll do just fine."

"Thanks, Dad." Jake sighed. His father was always telling him things he already knew.

Sisko put out his right hand. "I guess I'll see you in a week. Good luck."

It felt a little awkward to shake his father's hand. But it felt good, too, as if Jake had gained additional respect in his father's eyes. He could tell that Commander Sisko was proud of him.

"I'll miss you, Dad," Jake said.

Sisko released his hand, then drew his son into a hug. "I'll miss you, too, Jake."

Jake glanced nervously at the waiting shuttle. Kwiltek and Nog had disappeared inside. "I'd better get going."

"One last thing," Sisko said sternly.

Jake looked up at his father. "What, Dad?"

Sisko smiled. "Have fun. That's an important part of doing a good job."

Jake grinned. "Don't worry, Dad, I will!" Then he hurried off to the shuttle, where Kwiltek and Nog waited for him.

The mining company's huge mothership was a two-hour trip beyond the point where the Wormhole dumped them into the Gamma Quadrant.

The ship was enormous, like an industrial city in space, consisting of a series of long cargo sections with docking ports. Peering out the shuttle's viewport, Jake could see some kind of automated cargo container landing on a platform—probably one of the ore haulers that Kwiltek had mentioned, arriving from the surface of the planet.

The big, round planet below was misty white with pale lavender showing through the cloud cover. To Jake, it looked like a habitable class-M planet.

"On the contrary," Kwiltek said after Jake had mentioned his observation. "It's very hostile. There are rough mountains and deep canyons, as well as jagged forests of crystal that are almost impossible to navigate. You can even see some of the terrible lightning storms that rage across the surface from up here. Absolutely deadly. You'll get a better idea of what it's like when you actually get to the telepresence simulators. But don't worry—it's not dangerous for you."

"I hope it isn't boring," Jake said.

"Ah!" Kwiltek held up a leathery hand. "We have done everything we can to make your job more interesting. I think you'll particularly like how we spice up the routine drudgery of the mining work by staging simulated attacks. You'll find it to be similar to some of your video games."

Jake and Nog looked at each other in delighted anticipation.

Working the controls smoothly with his horned hands, Kwiltek guided their shuttle toward the front section of the mothership. The docking-bay door opened like a giant mouth, revealing a yawning, dark hole into which they flew. It took several minutes for the bay door to cycle shut, and then they had to wait for air to be pumped in.

"Please put these on," Kwiltek said to the boys after they had disembarked from the shuttle. He handed each

28

of them a tiny metallic disk emblazoned with the company logo.

"What is it?" Nog asked. He squinted at the metal disk, examining it more closely, as if it might be valuable.

"Life-support badges," Kwiltek said.

"Life-support? What do we need these for?" Jake said uneasily. He didn't like the sound of it.

Kwiltek's beak bobbed up and down. "In case there's an emergency on the facility. We want to be sure everyone is protected."

"You said we weren't in any danger," Nog said, quickly pinning the badge to the front of his shirt. "If we are, we expect to be compensated for hazardous duty."

"I assure you, it's quite safe. There's nothing to worry about." Kwiltek turned abruptly, his scale-feathers glittering in the dim light as he strode to a door on the far side of the shuttle bay.

"Let's hope not," Jake muttered under his breath as he and Nog followed.

"Please hurry," Kwiltek said with a nasal whistle. "We are behind on our production schedule, and we can't spare a lot of time to train you."

Jake and Nog glanced at each other as they hurried down a corridor after Kwiltek. The lights in the narrow, curving hall flickered eerily, reflecting from the metallic walls. Water dripped from a broken seal in one pipe; rust spotted the walls and floor. Everything looked old and in a bad state of disrepair.

Jake could see why Kwiltek had given them life-support badges. The mothership was in almost as bad shape as Deep Space Nine had been when his father had taken over command of the space station from the departing Cardassians. The Cardassians had stripped the station bare and even sabotaged some of the equipment. It had taken Chief O'Brien a lot of time and hard work to get the station livable.

Nog wrinkled his nose. "It stinks in here," he said in a low voice.

"Yeah." Jake was beginning to wonder if perhaps his father was right, that working here wasn't going to be as much fun as Kwiltek had made it out to be.

Jake's heart sank again as he saw the telepresence room. It was twice as big as the Arcade on Deep Space Nine, but the simulators looked a lot less sophisticated. About a hundred of them were crammed into the huge, gloomy room.

The simulator stations were partially enclosed control consoles with two pilot chairs set in front of a heads-up display. Pairs of kids worked the controls together. Jake watched the pair closest to him—a Bajoran girl about his age and a Benzite boy. Wisps of whitish gas rose from the breathing apparatus attached to the Benzite's chest.

The Bajoran girl's hands darted across the controls with amazing agility. Jake had never seen anyone that good in the Arcade. He wasn't sure *he* could match the speed with which she maneuvered the image of the flyer on the screen.

"Awww, we have better graphics than this in the Deep Space Nine Arcade," Nog whined.

A warble that might have been a sigh escaped Kwiltek's nostrils. "We have discovered that better simulators are not cost-effective. They do not increase productivity as much as better mining equipment does. We would rather invest credits where the return will be the greatest. You can do your job with these."

"That makes sense," Nog said, baring his teeth in agreement. "Cost-effective."

Jake walked over to the nearest empty simulator station. The display screen was blank, but the controls on the console glowed in readiness. Jake's fingers twitched in anticipation. He turned back to Kwiltek. "When can we get started?" He was anxious to see if he could match the Bajoran girl's skill.

"Right now," Kwiltek said, gesturing toward the seats with one hand. "Sit down, and I'll do a quick run-through to familiarize you with the procedure and the controls. It's really quite user-friendly."

"They look pretty simple," Nog said eagerly, scrambling into the seat next to Jake.

Kwiltek ran them through a quick training simulation. The mining machines had two separate components that worked together: an excavator-processor that moved on treads across the ground, and a finder-pulverizer that flew ahead, locating ore deposits and uncovering them with disrupter blasts.

Both machines had phasers to defend against the simulated attacks from fighters, missiles, and land mines that added excitement to the work. In addition, there were physical obstacles to be avoided: mudslides

31

and hidden pits. The terrain was a digitized schematic, relayed from the surface, that showed what the real ground looked like. Possible ore deposits were displayed as different-colored areas on the screen.

As soon as the remote-controlled excavator was full, the ore would be unloaded into a hauler for eventual transport up to the mothership.

"The goal," Kwiltek said, "is to excavate, process, and unload the greatest amount of ore in the shortest time, while sustaining the least amount of damage to your equipment." His beaked face showed no expression, though by his mannerisms he seemed to be smiling. "The team with the highest score at the end of its shift doubles its pay."

Nog's eyes widened, and he fidgeted impatiently. "What are we waiting for?" he said. "Let's get going, Jake! We've already lost a lot of time to everyone else here."

"Don't worry," Jake said confidently. "We'll catch up." He glanced at the other kids, especially the Bajoran and the Benzite, whose score was already higher than everyone else's. From the look of things, he and Nog had a lot of work to do.

"I hope you're right," Nog said. "If we can earn twice as much as my father and uncle counted on, I might get to keep the half they didn't anticipate."

"Hey," Jake said encouragingly, patting his friend on the shoulder. "We're the only ones who ever completed the 'Escape Through the Wormhole,' remember?"

Nog grinned.

"Good luck, you two," Kwiltek said. "I'll check in later, to see how you're doing."

"I'll operate the flyer," Jake said when Kwiltek was gone. That was what the Bajoran girl had been operating. "You take the excavator."

Nog made a face. "How come I always get the dirty work?"

Jake shrugged. "Maybe because you're so good at it?" He laughed.

"Very funny," Nog said. Then the two of them set to work, aiming for the highest score.

CHAPTER 4

Working the simulator controls, Jake circled his flyer low over a thick cluster of jagged lines that represented the huge crystal forests covering the surface of the planet.

The flyer was a crude, oblong blip on the display screen. Nog's slow-moving excavator showed as a long rectangle beneath it. To his right, the jagged outline of a mountain range rose like a series of pyramids above the horizon.

The overhead view gave Jake the exact location of rich deposits of titanium, gold, and duranium. Though it was only their second shift on the job, Jake already had become quite familiar with the way the system worked. The titanium was color-coded blue, the gold yellow, and the duranium red. Just about every other valuable mineral he could imagine was represented on the screen in a different color. Despite its hostile conditions, this was a rich world indeed—and the simulated attacks added plenty of fun to the hours of tedious work.

"Let's head for that canyon over there," Nog said. "Look at all the ore deposits in it."

"Yeah, but look at how dangerous it might be," Jake said. Rough terrain meant a bigger chance of ambush from the simulated enemy flyers. It also would be harder to pilot a flyer between V-sloped canyon walls than to control an excavator with treads.

"Nothing risked, nothing gained," Nog said. "Do you want to end up like we did this morning?"

Jake shook his head. "You're right, Nog," he said. "If we're going to come in in first place, we have to take chances."

The skilled Bajoran girl certainly did, and Jake had heard that she achieved the highest score most of the time. Jake was determined to beat her, though. At least he and Nog hadn't come in in last place in their first session—but they hadn't been close to winning, either.

Jake had stared at their score posted on the big screen at the end of their first shift. He lowered his head, disappointed, while the Bajoran girl and the Benzite boy calmly congratulated each other. It looked as if they were used to winning.

Nog hadn't made it any easier with his grumbling. "If you had come back to help me navigate out of that mine field, we wouldn't have had so many points deducted for damage." The Ferengi boy shook his head and hissed in disgust.

"If I'd come back," Jake countered, "we wouldn't have had time to get that last deposit."

"A lot of good it did us when I couldn't even get there!"

They had argued about it until the Bajoran girl came over, and embarrassment had silenced them both. "You didn't really expect to win your first time out, did you?" the girl asked.

Jake shrugged, then smiled sheepishly. "I guess I thought we'd do better than we did."

"I felt the same way when I first got here." The Bajoran smiled. "My name's Dobb, by the way. We didn't have time for introductions this morning."

"I'm Jake. This is my friend Nog. We're from Deep Space Nine."

"How long have you been here, girl?" Nog said, pushing past Jake to talk to her.

Dobb had long brown hair tied in a ponytail, and beautiful brandy-brown eyes. A stylized silver ear cuff with dangling chains was fastened to her right ear. She seemed a little thin to Jake. He wondered if she had come from one of the refugee camps on Bajor.

Jake tried to imagine what it must have been like to survive the Cardassian occupation of her planet. The war had devastated that world and its economy. He could see why she was working for Kwiltek now. It was probably the best way Dobb could earn a living.

"I've been here a little less than three months," Dobb said. "So has my partner, Tandon. We've had a lot of practice."

"Any tips on how to win?" Jake asked.

"None that I'm going to tell," Dobb said—but she smiled when she said it.

Jake shrugged. "Oh, well, it was worth a try. I guess we'll just have to beat you without any help."

"Hah! You may be good, but you're not *that* good," Dobb said.

"We'll see about that, girl!" Nog sputtered. "I'll wager we're just as good as you are. Better."

Dobb had shaken her head with a laugh. Jake remembered her words clearly from this morning: "It's been a long time since anyone's scored higher than we have. We're the best."

Not if I can help it, Jake now told himself, concentrating on the screen in front of him. He tightened his grip on the flyer controls, determined to prove her wrong.

A volley of simulated surface-to-surface missiles streaked toward Jake's flyer. He jerked the controls to one side, barely avoiding the warheads spreading out around him, then locked his phasers onto the missiles and fired. Explosions blossomed across the screen.

"That was close!" Nog shouted.

Jake wiped his brow. "Sorry."

"You should pay better atten—" Nog yelped in surprise as another explosion dislodged a huge rock from the cliff above. The Ferengi boy pulled back on the control stick, bringing his excavator to a halt. The boulder came to rest just in front of the big excavator, wedging between the narrow walls of the canyon.

"I'm not the only one who needs to pay better attention," Jake chided.

"Now what?" Nog asked, frustrated. "It's too big to fit

inside the excavator. We're going to lose valuable time. And time is money."

"Use your phasers to break it apart," Jake suggested.

"Oh, yeah . . . sure. I knew that." The excavator backed up, and its turret turned, bringing disrupters to bear. The rock vanished from the screen, broken up into chunks too small to register.

Jake risked a quick peek behind him at the simulator station where Dobb and Tandon were working. The score above their display screen read several hundred points higher than the tally in front of Jake. He and Nog didn't have much time left, less than an hour. If they didn't do something spectacular fast, they were going to come up short.

He watched the Bajoran girl execute a nifty maneuver that put her in position to take out two simulated missiles that were about to strike Tandon's excavator, which was burrowing into a duranium-rich deposit.

Out of the corner of his eye, he saw three triangular needle-nosed attack fighters appear out of the exotic crystals below. The sleek craft angled sharply toward him, closing distance faster than he expected.

"I'm being tracked!" Jake said. He yanked the control stick back. His flyer darted skyward. One of the fighters fell away, deciding to go for Nog's excavator.

"You'll have to get that one yourself, Nog," Jake said, focusing on the two fighters still tracking him.

"I'll get it!" Nog said, working his own controls furiously.

Jake twisted his swift flyer to the right, then dove. The tops of the crystals rushed up at him with dizzying speed. At the last possible instant, Jake leveled the flyer out, grazing the crystal canopy.

But the two attack fighters mimicked his maneuver perfectly. If anything, they had gained on him.

"I can't shake them!" Jake said, not daring to tear his gaze from the screen.

Nog made no reply, but Jake could hear the Ferengi's breath rasping with effort next to him. Nog had his hands full, too.

Jake zigzagged back and forth above the crystal tops, dipping up and down. Nothing seemed to work. "Can you help me yet, Nog?" he asked. If he could circle back and fly low, the excavator's phaser cannon could take out at least one of the attackers, maybe both.

"I'm busy!" Nog said. "Don't talk to me." He sounded desperate.

Jake wet his lips. His palms were sweaty against the control stick.

A large crystal suddenly loomed in front of him. Jake twisted the flyer to the left, barely missing the obstacle. Both fighters tracking him pulled away.

Jake breathed a sigh of relief—just as a fourth attack fighter darted out of the crystal lattice ahead of him. It had been hiding there, waiting. The crystal maze in this area must be filled with them!

Panic clenched Jake's stomach. There was no place to go . . . except down. He jammed the control stick forward, ducking under the new attack fighter—and right into the crystal latticework. It ripped at the wings of the flyer, jerking the craft from side to side.

He headed for a deep ravine a hundred meters ahead.

The walls squeezed narrowly together, but at least there would be no jagged crystals to contend with. The screen showed a small stream along the bottom.

Maybe.

Jake shoved the throttle to full as soon as he came out of the crystal forest and dropped into the steep-walled ravine. The fighter followed him down, right on his tail. He had to time it just right.

Jake held his breath. He didn't have much time. Ahead of him, the ravine narrowed and twisted. He wouldn't be able to pilot his way through the turns, not at the speed he was going. And he couldn't slow down. The fighter on his tail was too close.

It's now or never, Jake thought. Gritting his teeth, he targeted a spot on the tiny stream and locked his phasers on.

Three . . . two . . . *one!*

Jake fired his phasers, at the same time feeding every ounce of power to the flyer's engines. He saw the phasers score a direct hit on the water just as his flyer swept over the spot. An explosion of steam detonated behind him, billowing up from the river and engulfing the pursuing fighter.

When the clouds of steam evaporated from Jake's display screen, the fighter was gone. Jake let out a whoop.

"What happened?" Nog demanded in a sharp voice. "Was it good? I hope it was good."

"Steam," Jake said, laughing. "I used my phasers to superheat that river, and the sudden vaporization wiped out the ship chasing me."

"Risky," Nog said. "It could have gotten you."

"But it didn't," Jake said. Then he noticed Dobb giving him a sidelong glance, a faint smile tugging one corner of her mouth.

"Back to work," Nog said. "There's no profit basking in past accomplishments."

Jake circled his flyer back to Nog's excavator. "I'm going to go for the vein of duranium in the side of that mountain," he said, hoping that no more fighters were lurking in the crystals.

"But what if you bring the whole mountain down? I could be buried alive! Why not go for that pocket of gold farther away from the cliff face?"

"We're running out of time," Jake said. "If we don't score some big points fast, Dobb will beat us again."

Nog said dubiously, "It looks awfully dangerous."

"Nothing risked, nothing gained," Jake quoted. "Remember who said that?"

Nog squirmed in his seat. "The situation was different then."

"Yeah," Jake said. "That time, *I* was the one in the hot seat."

"All right," Nog finally agreed. "Just be careful."

"No problem," Jake said. "Watch this." He banked the flyer in a tight turn and swooped in low, weaving his way between scattered crystal growths as he approached the side of the mountain.

As Jake swept close to the cliff face, he fired a quick disrupter burst at the base of the deposit, hoping to blast away just enough of the surface rock to uncover and dislodge the rich minerals beneath. If he did it exactly right, the deposits would slide down the side of the mountain to where Nog waited with the excavator. Easy pickings, compared to the usual time it took to dig a strip mine or tunnel beneath a hill to reach a vein of metal.

The rippling beam gouged the mountainside. Jake imagined rock exploding and rubble flying as he pulled away hard to avoid an outcropping just beyond the ore deposit.

"It didn't work," Nog said. "Nothing is sliding down."

Jake frowned. "I must not have given it a powerful enough burst." He gripped the controls and brought the flyer around for a second pass.

"It's not going to work," Nog said nervously. "We should move on to an easier deposit, before we waste all our time pursuing a fruitless venture."

"It'll work," Jake said. "Trust me."

Beside him, Nog grimaced. His pointed teeth flashed in the flickering light from the simulator screens.

"You'd better hurry," Nog said. "Otherwise, we won't have time to make it back to the ore hauler. Then we'll lose lots of points."

Jake ignored his friend, concentrating on the screen in front of him. He targeted the disrupters on the same spot, then swept in at the same angle.

"Here it comes! Look out!" Nog yelled.

Jake pulled away, avoiding the rock outcropping.

Nog fired the excavator's disrupters in blind panic,

trying to pick off stray boulders that looked as if they might strike him. But the closest ones landed a hundred meters in front of the excavator.

Nog let out a sharp breath. "We did it!" The Ferengi boy cackled from the sudden release of tension, then clasped both clawed hands together in anticipation of all the raw duranium they would add to their score.

Jake peeked at Dobb's score. He and Nog had narrowed the gap. They were less than one hundred points behind. It would all depend on which team brought the most valuable cargo of ore back to the hauler.

"We won!" Nog cried gleefully. "I knew we could do it! You and me!" He clapped Jake happily on the arm. "Double pay, and half of it's all mine."

Jake grinned as the realization sank in. He hadn't fully appreciated how important it was for Nog to win. Unlike Jake, the Ferengi boy probably would see very little of his earnings if they didn't get the highest score. Quark or Rom would end up "investing" Nog's regular pay in some private scheme.

But all the risks they'd taken had paid off. Today, anyway. Tomorrow might be a different story. Still, it felt good to win.

Jake glanced at Dobb and Tandon. The Benzite stomped off in disgust, gases streaming from his breath mask. Jake felt bad for him, but not too bad. Benzites had a reputation for thinking they were better than everyone else. At least Dobb didn't look too upset. She walked over and smiled grudgingly. "Congratulations."

"Thanks," Jake said. "I guess we got lucky."

"Some of it was luck," Dobb admitted, "but not all of it. You pulled some crazy stunts down there. Especially that river steam maneuver."

Jake wasn't sure if she was complimenting him or not. He hoped she was. "I saw you do some pretty crazy things, too."

Dobb shrugged. "Most of the time, those only get you in trouble. But not always. Sometimes taking risks is the only way to win."

Jake got the impression she was speaking from first-hand experience—and not just when it came to working the simulators. Bajorans had become used to taking risks and accepting the consequences during their struggle against the Cardassians.

"See you tomorrow," Dobb said. "Don't expect to win again."

"You, either," Jake said.

Dobb laughed, then walked away. Jake had the feeling that she was looking forward to the competition.

CHAPTER 5

We really showed Dobb today," Nog said as he and Jake walked back to their quarters after their gaming shift. "That river steam maneuver you used to get away from the fighter was great. If we keep playing like that, I'll be rich in no time!"

Jake raised his eyebrows. "Rich?" he said. "Just because we doubled our wages today, I wouldn't call us rich anytime soon."

Nog blushed. "Oh, uh," he stammered. "I also made a few bets with some of the other players—that you could outscore Dobb, I mean. I saw an opportunity for profit."

"Profit?" Jake said, feigning severity. "I'm helping you make a profit without knowing it?"

Nog rubbed his clawed hands together, a worried look on his face. "I didn't want to put pressure on you, Jake," he said. "Besides, I've been planning to split the winnings with you all along. Say, thirty-seventy?"

Jake had to look straight ahead to keep from laughing. "Seventy percent for me? I can live with that."

"Seventy . . . ?" Nog said, dazed. "No, I meant seventy for *me*—"

Cut short by Jake's uncontrollable laughter, Nog muttered under his breath, "You humans have no respect for profit."

The boys fell silent as a Gorn mercenary guard from the mining corporation approached, a tall alien with a face like an Earth lizard and eyes like gold jewels. The Gorn glared suspiciously at them as it walked by, then turned a corner.

When they reached the door of their room, Jake sighed heavily. "I'm not really tired yet," he said. "Do you want to get something to eat with the other gamers?"

"Well . . ." Nog said, and Jake knew the Ferengi boy was wondering if he could drink a fourth Antarian shake in one day. Nog's stomach gurgled unhappily. "Maybe in a little while. You know, the food here is so extravagant. The mining company's profits must be very good. If my Uncle Quark opened a cantina here—"

"Kwiltek wouldn't let Quark on board," Jake said. "He'd be too afraid your uncle would take over."

Nog grinned slyly. "Yes . . . I'll have to mention that to my uncle. He'll be most interested."

Jake looked up and down the dim, metallic corridors. The dark paneling absorbed all the light so that the halls were even more dreary than on Deep Space Nine— perfect for exploring.

"Hey," Jake said, "why don't we go to the cargo bay? The next shift is bringing in the ore haulers right now. We've been filling those things for days, and I'd like to see what they look like."

"A box with thrusters," Nog said, yawning. "What's so exciting about that?"

"Come on," Jake coaxed. "I bet they're really interesting. We might even see some of the valuable ore we've been mining."

All traces of weariness vanished from Nog's face. His little Ferengi eyes sparkled with interest.

"Besides," Jake said, walking slowly down the corridor, "doesn't one of the Rules of Acquisition say something about getting to know your customer?"

"Rule Number 87," said Nog, following Jake eagerly.

"You checked the schematics of the mothership, didn't you? I haven't had a chance to study them yet," Nog said as he and Jake wandered uncertainly through the maze of corridors. "What if we're lost?"

"We're almost there," Jake said, although he really wasn't sure. The corridors all looked alike. *Functional,* as his father might have said. And even if he and Nog did find the cargo bay, Jake didn't know how they were going to find their way back to their quarters; but he wouldn't tell Nog that. Not until after Jake had had a chance to see the ore haulers in action.

The friends turned down one corridor, ducking quickly into a doorway to avoid another reptilian Gorn guard. The alien strode past without looking at them with its faceted eyes. Nog peeked out of the doorway. "There seem to be a lot more guards in this part of the ship," he said.

Jake nodded. "Probably worried about pirates transporting in to steal the ore," he said. "Let me know when the corridor is clear."

Nog leaned out again, then motioned for his friend to follow. After several meters, the two had to duck into another doorway to avoid two Andorian guards. Only seconds after the blue-skinned aliens with antennas and white hair marched past, Jake and Nog had to duck back into the same doorway to avoid one more set of guards, a female Andorian and a Gorn.

The Gorn hissed something at his companion. The Andorian calmly drew a phaser and said, "You can stop complaining and take the matter up with Kwiltek . . . or you can be quiet—permanently. The choice is yours."

"Kwiltek," the reptilian guard growled in a low, raspy voice.

The Andorian nodded and put her phaser away. As they passed the boys' hiding place, the Gorn touched his own phaser absently.

"I don't think I want to take any matter up with either of them," Nog whispered.

The two boys crept down the corridor, keeping close to the walls and listening for other footsteps. They ducked into doorways, hiding in the deep shadows. Most of the guards were surly Gorns or Andorians, although they narrowly avoided a tough-looking Klingon who wore a deep, savage scowl. Jake and Nog waited long after the Klingon's footsteps had faded before venturing out.

They finally reached a huge rectangular gateway guarded by a crosshatch of deadly red lasers. An access grid glowed bright orange at the center of the door. Nog and Jake backed into the nearest alcove to think.

"We'll never get in there," Nog said in defeat. "I'd bet you those lasers aren't set on stun."

"Yeah," Jake said, staring at the door in frustration. The lasers had to be pretty deadly for the mining company to leave the gateway otherwise unguarded, especially considering how many guards patrolled the corridors.

Jake studied the gateway but saw no way in unless they could figure out the security code. He frowned, wishing that he was a shape-shifter like Odo. Then he could just ooze under the door and let Nog in from the other side.

Just then, two Andorian guards approached. Nog ducked into the shadows, but Jake leaned forward as far as he dared, hoping to spot the security code by watching over the guards' shoulders. The first Andorian, his cool, calculating expression accentuated by a scar between his antennas, grasped his partner by the sleeve and thrust the other's arm toward the lasers. The second Andorian screamed, wrenching free. His sleeve smoked where the lasers had charred the cloth.

"Disobey me again in front of Kwiltek," said the first Andorian coolly, "and you can be sure I'll push more than your sleeve under those lasers."

"But Kwiltek hired us—" the second Andorian said.

"Kwiltek may have hired us, but I am still your commanding officer," sneered the first Andorian. "Don't you ever forget that."

Jake swallowed and looked at Nog, whose eyes widened with alarm. "Let's go back to our quarters," the Ferengi boy whispered. "There is no profit in getting killed."

"No kidding," Jake whispered. He held his breath, still watching the two Andorians.

"Open it," commanded the first guard. "Open it now, or I won't wait for you to disobey me in front of Kwiltek."

The second Andorian balked, then nodded stiffly, turning to the grid. Counting to himself, he pointed to each horizontal beam of light. Jake held his breath. The guard stopped at line seven, hesitated, then stuck his arm through the beam and pressed the glowing orange access grid.

The lasers winked out, and the door to the cargo bay opened. The scarred Andorian smiled. "Very good," he said. "Now, hurry, before it reactivates."

As soon as the door closed behind the two guards, Nog stepped out into the corridor. "Let's get out of here," he said.

But Jake's curiosity was even stronger now. "What are they hiding in there?" he said. "Why are they guarding it so heavily? They're not telling us something important. Come on, we need to find out what it is."

Nog shook his head. "But why? We don't need to find out anything—"

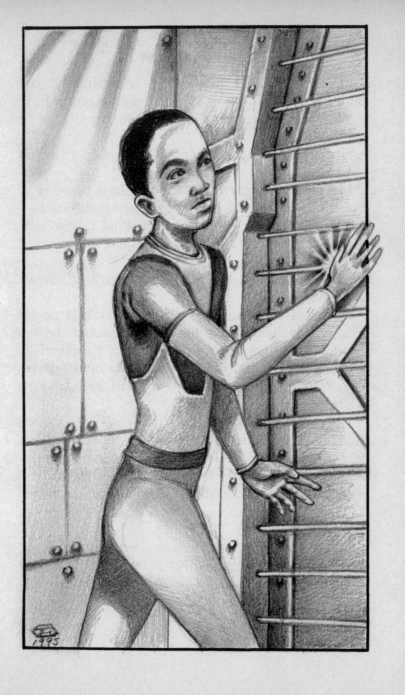

"Don't you want to know what's so profitable?" Jake said. "With this kind of security, they might even be mining pure latinum or dilithium and not giving us a percentage."

Nog's eyes lit up. "Latinum? Why didn't you say so?"

Making sure the corridor was clear, the two boys crept over to the door. Jake counted the horizontal lasers—twice—then motioned for Nog to stand to one side. "Stay out of sight," he said, "in case there's a guard just inside the door."

Nog nodded. "Hurry!" he said urgently. "Before someone comes!"

Jake thrust his arm through the seventh laser. He flinched involuntarily as his fingers touched the red beam. Nothing happened—no shock, no burning pain. A decoy. He reached in and pressed the orange access grid. Pulling his hand back, he leaped to the side as the door slid open.

The two boys peeked into the cargo bay. Not a guard in sight. They darted past the closing door and hid behind a vat that had thick, clawed arms. Just in time—as they hurried around the bottom of the vat, a Gorn guard rushed to the already closed door, phaser drawn. A small, furry creature, possibly a Bajoran crevice rat, dashed past the door.

The guard vaporized the rodent with a quick shot, then pocketed the weapon. "False alarm," he hissed. He walked away, disappearing behind a large, pitted machine that had spindly legs. Jake squinted at the odd mechanical shapes scattered throughout the dim cargo bay.

A flyer hovered on its side between three antigrav lifts. Jake could see that its underside had been blown open, leaving a metallic gash. Other strange machines, some with heavy blades like mandibles, hunched beside the giant storage bins that lined the walls. Alien workers scurried around the odd equipment like Garanian Bolites over some unsuspecting host.

The scarred Andorian captain and his partner walked up to a worker tinkering with the fiber optics on the damaged flyer. The scarred Andorian pointed toward the machine to the right of the vat where Jake and Nog crouched.

Jake ducked quickly out of sight, but Nog jabbed him in the ribs. "You were right," the Ferengi boy said in a hushed, reverent tone. "Look!"

Peeking around the side of the vat, Jake looked to where his friend pointed. A gigantic gray box stood in the middle of the cargo bay. A worker using an antigrav lift stood beside it, cranking the box's top back to reveal a load of raw, unprocessed latinum.

"Wait till I tell Uncle Quark!" Nog whispered. "He owes me a bonus for this!"

But Jake hardly saw the latinum. He was too busy gaping at the ore hauler. Nog had been right in calling it a box with thrusters—a very battered and scarred box with rounded corners, except that one of the corners jutted outward in jagged fangs of damaged metal, a little like Nog's teeth.

Something crusty was splattered on the base of the

automatic pilot where it attached to the front of the box, nearly obscuring the ore hauler's optics. Jake shook his head. This wasn't the normal wear and tear of space travel. The dents and gouges were too deep. The ore hauler had *really* been attacked and damaged—many times.

"But the enemy fighters in the game were supposed to be imaginary!" Nog said.

Jake grabbed Nog's arm. "Let's get out of here," he said.

The other boy yearned toward the ore hauler with its gleaming cargo. "I've never been in the presence of so much latinum," he said worshipfully. "Just a minute longer. I want to remember this."

"Hey!" someone shouted. "You're not supposed to be in here!"

Jake and Nog turned to find themselves looking into the phaser of the Gorn guard.

"Run!" Jake shouted.

The boys ducked behind the vat, out of the line of fire, then ran as fast as they could. Although machines crowded the cargo bay, providing some cover for the fleeing boys, workers and guards also crawled everywhere in the bay. Jake darted behind an overturned machine with jawlike blades, searching frantically for a place to hide. Nog spurted ahead and ducked behind a storage bin. Jake dived in after him.

Footsteps raced past their hiding place. Jake pressed his lips together, hoping his ragged breathing wouldn't give them away.

From about ten meters away, the scarred Andorian
called out, "Split up! You two—go that way. You two—
over there. You—you're with me. The rest of you—
check behind the storage bins. We can't let them escape!"

A phaser sizzled several meters away. Heavy footsteps
ran toward the boys' hiding place, then stopped.

Jake closed his eyes, bracing himself for the inevitable
phaser blast. It didn't come. Instead, Nog jabbed him in

57

the ribs. Jake opened his eyes. Nog pointed wildly at an air duct less than a meter away.

Quickly, they removed the screen and plunged down the shaft. "Pull it closed behind us!" Jake whispered frantically.

Nog nodded and pulled the screen back into place. Less than a second later, a phaser blast whizzed past the vent. Jake and Nog froze. Another blast flashed by.

"Nothing behind this one!" someone shouted. Footsteps raced away.

Jake let out a long-held breath. Nog did the same, then jerked his head toward the dim depths of the air duct. Jake nodded. It wasn't until they had crawled well out of earshot of the cargo bay that either of them spoke.

"We've got to find Kwiltek," Jake said. "We need to tell him what's really going on."

CHAPTER 6

Nog stopped at an intersection of two air ducts, panting after their cramped flight through the maze of murky passages. He looked over his shoulder at Jake. "Don't tell me," he said. "You want to go up again."

Jake nodded and crawled over to sit next to Nog. "If I remember right, the command center is on the third level," Jake said. "That's where Kwiltek will be." He took a deep breath and exhaled heavily. "Let's rest for a minute. I think we're between floors. I doubt anybody will be able to hear us."

Nog slumped against the wobbly metal side of the air duct. "So long as no one shoots at us again," he said. He smiled, a dreamy expression on his face. "Did you see all that latinum? Wasn't it beautiful?"

"Yeah, very pretty," Jake said impatiently. "But how do you explain the damage to the ore hauler? It looks like someone's been blasting at it."

Nog sat up straight. "But it's only a simulation, Jake. Nobody could live on a hostile planet like that one."

Jake frowned. "I don't know what to think. I'm beginning to wonder if any of this really is a game."

Nog pressed his lips together. "Maybe pirates are attacking the ore haulers as soon as they leave the surface. And maybe that Andorian guard is in on it. I bet that's why they wanted to get rid of us so badly. They're afraid we'll tell Kwiltek."

"Well, we *are* telling Kwiltek, as soon as we find him," Jake said, crawling past his friend. He grasped the handholds and pulled himself up. "We've got to talk to him before they destroy the evidence."

Nog followed Jake up the shaft, smiling eagerly now. "Maybe Kwiltek will pay us handsomely for the information," Nog said. "Maybe he'll even double our salary."

Quickly gaining the third level, the two boys crept along. Nog paused every now and then to eavesdrop when they came to a grille over a room. "Hey, how much did that provisioner just say she paid for Saurian brandy?" Nog asked, stopping near a vent in the galley complex. "I'm sure my uncle would be happy to supply the station at a fraction of the cost."

"Shhh! Quark isn't going to supply anybody with anything if we don't get out of here and find Kwiltek," Jake whispered.

Soon they reached the command levels of the mothership. Jake stopped at another intersection. "I can't remember enough of the ship's schematics," he said, glancing down the right branch of the air duct. "Do you think the command center would be to the right or the left?"

Nog hissed between his pointy teeth. "Left, I think."

Jake headed to the left, but they reached a dead end after only fifteen meters.

"I said, 'I think,'" Nog protested when Jake gave him an exasperated look.

They crawled back, tired and anxious, taking the other fork this time. As they approached a large vent opening, whistles and clicks drifted down the shaft. It reminded Jake of an educational holoprogram about birds he had once watched.

A loud, flutelike shrill rose above the others. "That sounds like Kwiltek," Jake said, hurrying toward the vent. "We've got to hurry."

When he stopped in front of the opening, Nog bumped into him from behind. The distant sounds of simulated explosions and whirring, chewing machinery joined the murmuring whistles. "Maybe they're playing the game themselves," Nog said.

The vent looked out two meters above the floor. Jake and Nog peered through the slatted barrier into the room below, but they could see only vague shadows and shapes. Three or four tall figures stood watching a big screen. One of the figures detached itself from the group and walked across the room. Tinny-sounding screams and shouts rang from the simulation speakers. One of the operators apparently had just scored big points.

The figures in the command room warbled and cackled. "Good, very good," said Kwiltek. "Reward Vesta and Rux with extra points for that one."

Nog's brow puckered thoughtfully. "I wonder if he awarded us extra points for your steam-explosion idea."

Jake shrugged, then grunted as he pushed at the vent with his shoulder, trying to nudge it loose. "Help me with this, will you? Boy, is Kwiltek going to be surprised."

The metal screen popped loose after two more shoves, but Jake hung on so it wouldn't clatter to the floor. He jumped out of the air shaft, landing in a squat. Nog dropped quietly to the floor beside him. Rising slowly, Jake looked around, still holding the screen in front of him. His heart pounded with anticipation.

Kwiltek stood tall in the center of the room, watching the show. His green scale-feathers bristled with excitement from his beaklike nose to the top of his head. Beside him waited two similar aliens, one with deep, midnight-blue scale-feathers and another with stubby, gray-green plumage. Another gray-green alien leaned over a console. Whistles and snaps filled the room as the aliens clicked their beak mouths excitedly.

All four aliens stared up at a huge, glowing wall screen that showed a lush purple-and-white jungle of ferns and tall palm trees with oval leaves. Condensed moisture dripped from vines dangling from the tangled branches on the screen.

Growling noisily, a huge machine with churning, clawlike scoops chewed its way across the jungle landscape, leaving a scar of ravaged land in its wake. A battered mining company flyer, like the one in the mothership's cargo bay, hovered overhead, firing its phaser beam in front of the excavator.

Someone screamed in a wild, alien voice.

Suddenly, a band of slim humanoids broke from the jungle near the disrupted soil and fled. A four-winged creature, its iridescent wings glistening in the sun, dived, hurling something into the machine's clawlike blades before climbing toward safety. The creature threw back its sleek, triangular head to emit a breathtaking, beautiful cry.

Before the winged creature could escape, though, the flyer spun and blasted it out of the air with its phasers. One of the humanoids scrambled back on-screen, looking up at the sky and wailing in anguish.

Jake's stomach turned over at the realism of the scene. Beside him, Nog paled, gnashing his teeth.

Kwiltek and the other aliens cheered in their odd, chirping voices.

"Well done, Kwiltek," the midnight-blue alien said. "You have chosen your teams skillfully."

"Thank you," Kwiltek said, obviously pleased. "I am quite happy with this group of new recruits."

With a loud crash, Jake dropped the vent screen in his hand. "What—what is that?" he said, staggering forward. "Kwiltek, who are those people?"

The room erupted with startled whistles, warbles, and clicks as the aliens turned on Jake and Nog. Behind the aliens, the screen went blank for a split second, then reverted to the familiar crude triangles, ovoids, squares, and crystalline shapes Jake and Nog already knew so well from their own simulation games.

The midnight-blue alien shrieked at Kwiltek, who stood perfectly still, staring at the two boys. The membranes along his hardened beak flickered.

Nog caught at his friend's arm. "Jake, maybe we shouldn't have—"

Kwiltek silenced his fellow aliens with a glare, then swept toward Jake and Nog, grasped the necks of their tunics, and ushered them from the control room. "What are you doing here?" he demanded, shoving them into the corridor past two Andorian guards. "This is a restricted area."

"We, uh," Nog stammered, "we were looking for you."

"Yeah," Jake said. "We had to tell you—"

Kwiltek released them, then cocked his head to one side. The anger had vanished from his voice when he finally spoke. "If you wished to talk to me, you had only to ask the computer to contact me. I would have come to you at my earliest convenience. Now, what can I do for you?"

"We, uh . . ." Nog said, staring blankly at Kwiltek.

Jake tugged at his tunic, straightening the wrinkles from Kwiltek's rough handling. "Who were those people we saw on the screen?" he said. "And the jungle. What was that all about?"

Kwiltek inhaled with a hiss. "Those people? On the screen? Why, a simulation, of course. We are trying to develop more entertaining simulations for operators such as yourselves. We have been working on a scenario—a rainforest scenario—that will add greater excitement to what might otherwise become a boring exercise."

"But what about your profits?" Nog said, further wrinkling his already ridged forehead. "You said that the simple displays we're using are more cost-effective."

"And you said that better resolution wouldn't help our efficiency," Jake added.

"Ah," Kwiltek said with a fluting whistle. "We have found a way to provide better resolution and more entertaining scenarios for a fraction of the cost. And, because we are so impressed with this new team of operators—yourselves especially—we hope to keep you satisfied and interested. As I told you, we need good operators."

"The new resolution was great," Nog said enthusiastically. "It looked very real, much better than the Arcade screens on Deep Space Nine. If you'd like to sell a version of this program to the owner of the Arcade on the station, I'm sure I could arrange it. For a small fee, of course."

"Ah!" Kwiltek said, bobbing his head. "Perhaps at some future time. For now, this little scenario must be kept secret. To prevent others from stealing our ideas, you understand. Which is why my partners and I were so upset when you appeared in the command center. I'm afraid I will have to ask for your discretion in this matter."

Jake took a deep breath and opened his mouth, but before he could speak, Nog suggested, "It will be hard to keep such a great simulation to ourselves. Do you think we could test it sometime?"

"I quite understand, but it is still under development," said Kwiltek sympathetically. "If word of our trade secret gets out, we will be forced to dismiss those responsible for the leak."

Nog's jaw dropped. "You mean, you'd *fire* us?"

"Ah," Kwiltek warbled. "Such an ugly word! But *you* understand. To continue your employment under such circumstances would show poor business sense on my part."

"I agree," Jake said hastily, silencing Nog with a kick in the foot. "Just like losing machinery through clumsy accidents—which is why we were looking for you. We went to the cargo bay to see what the ore haulers looked like." He smiled what he hoped was an innocent smile and shrugged. "After operating them by telepresence and all, we were a little curious."

Kwiltek's scale feathers bristled. "Ah," he trilled.

Jake continued quickly. "But the hauler we saw looked pretty beat-up."

"Horrible," Nog said, shaking his head adamantly. "Dents, scratches, damage—"

"Like someone had been firing at it," Jake said. "With real weapons."

Kwiltek's head bobbed again with that odd jerking motion. He chuckled, a cross between a wheeze and a whistle. "Ah! Yes, the cargo crew told me. It seems the ore hauler encountered a meteor storm on the way back to the mothership. Meteor storms are infrequent, but they happen—one more reason we feel it would be too dangerous to send actual workers to the planet's surface. Imagine what might have happened if a real person had been piloting that ore hauler."

Neither boy had to fake a shudder.

"Now, if you'll excuse me," Kwiltek said, "I must return to the command center. And remember—not a word about the new simulation."

"Oh, we wouldn't dream of it," Jake said, still suspicious but pretending to agree.

"You can count on us," Nog answered, eyeing Jake. "You have our word."

"Good," Kwiltek said. "Why don't you boys go back to your quarters and rest before your next shift? I'll check in on you a little later to see how you're . . . adjusting."

Jake took Nog's elbow and steered him toward their quarters. "Come on, Nog," he said.

Nog turned one last time to grin and bow to Kwiltek with typical Ferengi deference. "A pleasure doing business with you, sir."

CHAPTER 7

Do you think Kwiltek believes us?" Nog asked anxiously as the door to their quarters whished shut behind them. "He could dock our pay if he felt we were trying to steal their trade secrets. We could lose all of our profits."

Jake's narrow face clouded with concern as he headed for the food synthesizer slot on the wall. "That's not what's bothering me."

Nog had noticed that in times of crisis, his human friend often fixed himself a snack. Perhaps Jake needed the extra energy to help him think.

"One vegaburger, hot, catsup and mustard, no relish, no onions," Jake said to the food replicator. "And two Antarian shakes, mixed fruit."

Jake looked Nog straight in the eye, handing him a shake. "The problem is, I don't know if I believe *Kwiltek,*" he said.

Nog almost dropped the Antarian shake. Jake continued, his face serious. "We saw some things that are just a little too suspicious—the real damage to the ore carrier, that detailed jungle simulation where people and animals were being destroyed. It looked too real to me."

That brought Nog up short. He had been more concerned with whether or not they would lose their lucrative, if temporary, positions with the mining company.

"You're right, Jake," he said, flashing his friend a sharp-toothed grin. "You know I never trust what anyone tells me—not even my own family."

The other boy rolled his eyes. *"Especially* not your own family."

"So what's your point?" Nog asked, taking another sip of his shake. It was refreshing and delicious, and he knew he could have another one if he wished. Jake took a bite of the juicy vegaburger and gulped his own Antarian shake. This place was too good to be true. *Too good to be true.* Putting down his drink with an abrupt *thunk,* Nog began to pace the room.

"Think about it," Jake said. "They haven't told us the whole truth about this mining operation. They didn't even tell us about the latinum, for instance. They said we were mining less valuable minerals."

Nog said scornfully, "They'd be fools to tell us. Pirates would be all over this world if they knew about that much latinum just waiting to be mined."

"But what else aren't they telling us about?" Jake persisted. "What about that jungle we saw? Sure looked real to me. And why was Kwiltek so upset about us seeing them? Don't you Ferengis have some sort of proverb about employers?"

"We have many."

"I mean something about covering things up with money."

Nog rubbed an ear ridge. "You mean, 'The hand that holds the latinum may also hide a dagger'?"

Jake chuckled. "That wasn't the one I was thinking of, but it'll do." He took another bite of his burger and wiped the juice from his hands. His face took on a worried look again. He swallowed hard. "What if Kwiltek has been lying to us all along? What if we don't know what we're really doing? Maybe they're just telling us kids what we want to hear."

Nog looked down at his shake. "And feeding us what we want to eat?"

"Yeah, that, too. So why did they really bring us here?"

Nog shrugged. "Because we're earning them millions of credits by mining latinum on a hostile planet? And because we're good at computer games."

"We're the best," Jake agreed. "But what if it's not a game? And what if it's not such a hostile planet after all?"

"We know the mining part is for real," Nog said defensively, then rubbed a blue fingernail along his lips, pondering. "But what about the fighting? What if all that stuff we saw on the simulator screens in the control room is real? What if we're shooting at real trees, real animals—real *people?*" Nog chewed on his lower lip.

"They could be running the actual pictures from the planet through video enhancement filters," Jake said, picking up the thread. "They told us they were using the game screens to add to our enjoyment. Hah! What's to stop them from converting the real images to colorful gaming screens, so that we don't think we're damaging someone else's planet? Kwiltek could make us see whatever he wanted us to." He swallowed hard again.

"With a strong motive like profit," Nog added thoughtfully, "they could be capable of almost anything."

Jake straightened up as if coming to a decision. "We have to find out," he said. "Come on."

"Where are we going?" Nog asked in alarm. "Kwiltek said to stay here! Are we going to try to find the video filters and disable them?"

"No, that would take too long," his friend said. "I have a better idea."

"I still think it's a bad idea," Nog growled, looking over the controls as Jake stood on the pad in the darkened transporter room. He looked around, half expecting a guard to barge in at any moment.

"I'll be fine," Jake assured him. "What could happen in fifteen minutes? Even if the atmosphere is as bad as they say it is, my life-support badge should protect me for that long." He tapped the badge on his chest. "I go down and look around, and you beam me back up."

Nog squinted down at the unfamiliar transporter

control panel. The backs of his ears tingled, and that wasn't a good sign. "Four minutes is the most I can leave you down there," he said.

Jake gave an exaggerated sigh. "Twelve minutes, Nog. This is important."

"Six minutes, but that's my best offer," Nog replied.

Jake shook his head. "I can't make it in less than ten."

"Eight minutes, and not a moment more," Nog snapped.

"Agreed."

Nog didn't bother to hide his satisfaction. Jake had learned much about negotiating. "Eight minutes, beginning now," he said, energizing the transporter. "Good luck, Jake."

He watched as Jake's form blurred and scintillated, like a cloud of Numidian glow-flies that faded away to nothingness. Nog locked the coordinates of Jake's beamdown point into the transporter's memory and set a countdown timer to alert him when he was supposed to beam Jake back up.

Seven minutes left, he thought. Well, they would not be wasted minutes; he would see what he could do for himself. Nog was a championship hologame player, after all.

Nog moved to the computer screen beside the transporter console. He pushed a button, and it flickered to life. Nog murmured, chuckling at his own resourcefulness. He tapped a few keys, and a small yellow light blinked at the corner of the input pad. The screen said:

ACCESS CODE?

He studied the keypad in front of him carefully and then pressed another button. The tiny light winked off, and the message on the screen said:

ACCESS OVERRIDE ACCEPTED
PLEASE CONTINUE

Nog rubbed his hands together in anticipation, limbering them up as he did when preparing for a very difficult session in the Arcade. Then, working his way along by intuition born of long practice at such things, he brought up level after level of diagrams and ship schematics. "Propulsion systems," he muttered, nodding as charts and maps flashed before his eyes. "Cargo bays, crew's quarters . . ."

He shot a quick glance over at the chronometer. Three and a half minutes left. *That should be more than enough,* he thought.

Nog looked back at the computer screen and called up the next schematic. It showed the sophisticated transmitters that sent codes from the gaming room down to the mining equipment on the planet below. His breath quickened, and he focused his entire attention on the monitor before him. "There!" he cried in triumph as he saw what he had been looking for. Jake was right! Kwiltek was doctoring the images.

He pressed a button to freeze the screen so he could study it better. Before him lay the schematics for the video links that received transmissions from the planet, shunted them through a series of video-effects filters, and then routed the altered images to the gaming consoles.

Two minutes left, Nog noted with glee, as he wondered what other information he could acquire before Jake returned.

Then he heard a whishing sound behind him. He whirled to see an Andorian guard striding through the

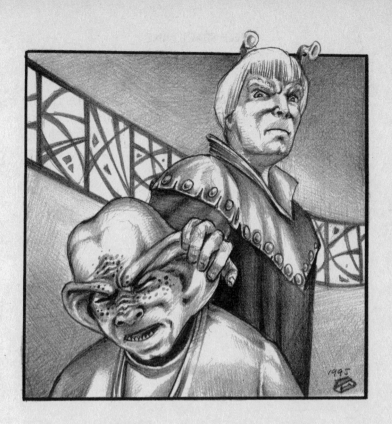

doorway with a hand-held phaser pointed directly at Nog's head. "Don't move," the guard said.

Nog's scrolled ear ridges contracted painfully, and he raised his hands. "Don't shoot me! I surrender!"

"You are in a lot of trouble, boy," the Andorian guard said, stepping to the transporter control panels, glancing down at them. His antennas quivered. "So, our Earth friend has made an unauthorized excursion to the planet." He punched in a code and flicked a switch. The countdown timer stopped dead.

The guard gave Nog an unpleasant smile. "His return ticket has just been canceled. And you," he said, grasping one of Nog's sensitive ear lobes with his free hand and twisting until Nog howled in pain, "have just been invited to tea with Kwiltek."

CHAPTER 8

The planet's surface took shape around Jake as he transported down. He felt a rush of warm, moist air on his face. A tiny pink moon shone brightly in the night sky, casting a rosy glow over the eerie landscape around him.

The steep, hilly terrain looked as if it had been attacked with a giant dull axe. Huge, jagged rips in the ground stood out on all sides, so deep that their bottoms were lost in misty shadows. Immense piles of crumbling, discarded rock stood next to each of the gashes. The destruction could only have been made by giant machines: remotely controlled excavators.

But in the midst of the ruined land stood islands of thick jungle that the video filters back in the mothership's game room had camouflaged. What those simulations had depicted as crystal canopies of minerals were actually lush growths of purple and ivory foliage. As Jake looked around the horrible, strip-mined landscape, he realized that rain forests had once covered the surrounding slopes.

Kwiltek had lied to them after all, just as Jake had suspected. What he and Nog had seen accidentally on the command center wall screen was real, not just a high-resolution simulation, as the alien had said.

Jake heard a growling, grinding sound in the near distance. He climbed a muddy rise until he looked down at a cluster of harsh white lights—the excavators chewing another slope, hungry for the raw ore buried underneath.

The lush, buzzing forests stood doomed before the machines. Jake had seen images of the giant automated miners on Kwiltek's wall screen, but he hadn't realized the excavators were so big!

Clawlike scoops dug deep into soil loosened by broad-beam phasers from the circling flyers. Other excavators worked relentlessly with a deafening grinding and roaring in the jungle night.

But what of the natives he'd seen on the command center screen, battling the machines? They also must be real, and they were engaged in a brave but futile fight to save their home. Jake scanned the surrounding hills, hoping to find some definite evidence of humanoid life before Nog beamed him back up to the mothership.

But Jake saw only ruined land and the shattered stumps of what had once been thick forests. Then, off in the distance, at the foot of a tall bluff, Jake spotted a band of spindly figures. In the pinkish moonlight, he could make out no features, couldn't even be certain that they were really humanoids. He had to make contact with them somehow, and he had to hurry before Nog beamed him back up. They might not get another chance.

Jake ran as fast as he could toward the clustered figures, through newly cut trenches and past torn slopes deeply eroded from rains. Jake stopped, panting for breath, and wondered why Nog hadn't beamed him up yet. Surely he'd been here longer than eight minutes.

Maybe Nog had relented and granted him a little extra time. Jake took off running again. But when he once more tired of the constant rugged terrain, he began to get worried. What was wrong with his friend? He couldn't believe Nog would leave him here so long.

Had the Ferengi boy gotten distracted by playing new simulation games on the main computer? Jake couldn't believe Nog would just forget about him. At least fifteen minutes had passed, almost twice the time they had agreed on—unless Nog couldn't help it. Maybe a guard had discovered him in the transporter room and taken him away to face Kwiltek's wrath.

If that's the case, Jake thought, *what's going to happen to me?*

He told himself not to think about that and started forward once again, skidding and running down an incline toward the natives. They stood silhouetted against a clump of forest as yet untouched by the mining machines.

The figures noticed him in the moonlight, pointed, and gestured to each other. Their mouths moved, but Jake couldn't hear a thing above the low-pitched roar of the excavators.

If Nog had been discovered and taken away, Jake was stuck here until Kwiltek chose to bring him back. Cold fear flowed like ice in Jake's veins. What if he had to spend the rest of his life on this ruined world? He might never see his father again, or Nog, or even Deep Space Nine.

Jake forced those thoughts from his mind. He had to act, do something useful. That's what his dad would have done under the circumstances. He had to reach the natives and see what he could find out. It was slow going as he fought his way up the steep slope, and the slippery mud squished under his feet. He fought his way closer to the humanoids, but every moment he expected to feel the buzzing, tingling sensation of the transporter.

It never came. With each minute, he lost hope for a simple rescue.

The planet's dawn broke over the horizon, a large red-orange sun emerging above the forest canopy. The sun was barely up before the air temperature began to warm noticeably.

As he approached the excited band of natives, Jake noticed several fuzzy spheres in their midst. The fur balls unexpectedly flew up into the air from time to time, then drifted back down again. No one seemed to throw them; they just took off on their own.

The slender natives waited to meet Jake, openly apprehensive as he approached. He knew that the Federation strictly followed its most important rule, the Prime Detective, which forbade any Federation citizen from interfering with other planetary societies. But, he thought angrily, Kwiltek's mining company was already interfering—no, they were *exploiting* this beautiful world. Kwiltek had already done plenty of damage, and it was up to Jake to help the natives somehow.

As he climbed over the lip of the gully, Jake finally came face to face with the inhabitants of this supposedly dead and hostile world.

Like a trapped animal, Nog paced his quarters, formulating a plan of action. He had to find some way to rescue Jake.

He was no longer chagrined that stony-faced Kwiltek had placed him under house arrest with an Andorian guard outside the door.

"You are dismissed from our employ," Kwiltek had said, setting down his narrow teacup, his emerald-green scale-feathers flattening against his beaked head. "No more profits for you. You will remain confined to quarters until I decide what to do with you."

Pleading and terrified, Nog had tried to assure Kwiltek that if they just brought Jake back from the surface, both he and the human boy would promise never to reveal the mining company's trade secret. But Kwiltek had not listened. The birdlike alien had not even been willing to negotiate.

What if Kwiltek was devising some awful way to ensure his silence? Staging a terrible accident? Or did Kwiltek have some kind of illegal machine to erase his memory? Nog shuddered at the thought of anyone tampering with his brain, erasing all the business knowledge he had compiled in the past fifteen years. He could be ruined for life.

He stopped abruptly at the food replicator slot, gnashing his sharp teeth. He was *not* about to let that happen.

"Antarian shake," he growled, "mixed fruit. Make that a double." Jake would have approved. *Jake,* he thought, taking a gulp of the shake when it appeared. He had to find a way to stop the mining machines down there before his friend got hurt. Nog had to rescue Jake from the hostile planet.

He smiled, relishing the challenge as his brain clicked into overdrive. He finished off the Antarian shake, set down the glass, and rubbed his hands together. He would make the mining company think twice about trying to profit at the expense of a Ferengi again!

Nog's door, still locked from outside, did not open at his approach. He placed one large, sensitive ear against the cool metal and listened. The Andorian guard outside shuffled his feet and coughed. Nog shrugged. Didn't Rule of Acquisition Number 92 say there were many paths to profit? He shook his head at the naïveté of the guard. There was *always* more than one path.

Mentally reviewing the diagrams of the mothership he had seen in the computer, Nog climbed onto his sleeping pallet and began to remove the brackets that held the cover of the air duct in place. He couldn't believe Kwiltek had been so sloppy, but Nog would take advantage of the opportunity. He knew exactly where he had to go and what he had to do.

CHAPTER 9

Jake had seen humanoids from hundreds of systems come through Deep Space Nine, but he had never seen a race as strikingly beautiful as the ethereal folk who now stood before him.

Even the tallest of the natives was half a head shorter than Jake. He was accustomed to many of the species on Deep Space Nine towering over him, but now *he* felt like the giant.

The natives were slender, with arms and legs so thin they looked fragile. Their skin was pink and very smooth, shiny like the surface of a fine ceramic vase. Their heads were round and devoid of hair except for a knot of fine, silky red strands sprouting from the crown and cascading down one side of the face. Around the base of this topknot, each native wore a band studded with sparkling blue stones.

Their noses, chins, and cheekbones were all delicately sculpted, giving them the look of carefully crafted dolls. Their eyes were huge and round, a gemlike blue that matched the bands around their topknots. At the natives' feet huddled the large furry balls Jake had seen before, now motionless.

All the natives wore sensible dress for the hot climate: sleeveless tunics that ended around mid-thigh. The fabric was woven from a soft brown material, the same shade as the fur on the bouncing spheres.

Jake greeted the small group, opening his hands to show that he carried no weapons. "I'm from the Federation station Deep Space Nine," he explained.

"What is a Federation?" one native asked in a surprisingly rich and deep voice for someone so tiny. The Universal Translator in Jake's comm badge picked up the alien's questioning tone.

Jake was amazed to meet someone who had never heard of the Federation, even here in the Gamma Quadrant. "It's a group of worlds that have joined together for mutual trade and protection."

Another of the natives turned to him and said incredulously, "There are other worlds besides our own?"

Still another looked beyond Jake, his face very angry as he pointed to the rumbling mining machines ripping apart the landscape. "Are those new monsters part of your Federation?"

When the native asked, the furry ball at his feet made a buzzing, growling sound and leaped back toward the protection of the forest. The furry ball was alive!

"Those are excavators," Jake answered. "They're not monsters. Just machines."

The natives turned their big blue eyes toward each other in confusion. "But how can they not be alive?" said the first one who had spoken. "Everything on Citra is alive—our forests, our mountains. How can dead things crawl through our forests, devouring them?"

"Living people guide them from a distance," said Jake. "They're the ones responsible."

"Like we oversee our bangas," mused the leader, looking down at one of the furry balls. "Why do people do such a thing? Why do they destroy our beautiful world?"

Jake swallowed, not wanting to justify the mining corporation's actions, just to explain them. "Because the metal they take out of the ground is worth a fortune. The latinum brings them great power back on their home worlds."

The leader shook his pink head, not understanding. His long red topknot switched from side to side. Another of the natives came forward, looking earnestly at Jake. Unlike the uniformly pink leader, this one—a female—had dark blue shoulders.

"You know about these excavator monsters? Can you stop them? So many of us have died." The girl looked at the torn-up dirt at her feet, shoulders slumping. "My mother fell into a monster's mouth as she tried to stop it from ripping through one of our fields. I will never forget her scream."

Jake's throat tightened with remembered hurt to hear

such a tale. He had lost his own mother when the Borg had attacked the Federation.

"I'm very sorry. I know a little about those machines. Perhaps I could help you fight them better. If you can propel a good-sized illurium shape charge into the excavator's—" he began. But the natives' blank expressions told him that they had no such thing as illurium. "Or perhaps a disrupter beam aimed at . . ." *No, I guess they don't have one of those, either.* "What weapons *do* you have?"

"Explosive gourds," said the native girl.

Jake sighed hopelessly, then realized that these gourd bombs must have been the explosive devices used to attack the excavators in the video games he and Nog had played for Kwiltek. And, though they seemed crude, when the bombs hit certain sensitive parts of an excavator, the primitive explosives had been pretty effective. If Jake could show these natives the best places to aim, perhaps he could help them stall the destructive mining, or even inflict enough losses to stop the operation completely.

If Jake could get back to the mothership and warn the other kids to stop playing the simulation games . . . Why hadn't he been beamed back up according to the plan? What had Kwiltek done with Nog? Would Kwiltek dare leave Jake stranded on this world forever?

He followed the native girl. As soon as they entered the thick, humid forest, they plunged into a twilight colored by the violet and ivory of the ferns and palm trees around them. Even the vines that hung from the tree branches were a deep, rich purple, dripping with moisture.

The collective mood of the three bouncing, furry bangas changed the moment they all entered the forest. Once out of sight of the excavators, the little creatures perked up as they hopped along, buzzing and purring.

The blue-shouldered girl fell into step beside Jake. "I am Tani," she said, raising a hand so that her palm faced him. He looked at her and then did likewise. Tani touched her fingertips to Jake's. She had to spread her small fingers wide apart to reach his.

"I'm Jake," he said. "Jake Sisko." He liked the way her red topknot covered one pink cheek as she walked, its strands rippling in the gentle breeze. It reminded him of a human girl's ponytail.

When they arrived at the Citranese village, Jake was surprised at its simplicity. Fifteen small buildings constructed of deep purple wood were scattered around a clearing in the forest. Jake paused to look more closely at the huts, but Tani impatiently motioned for him to follow.

"Look at those later. I want to show you our weapons." She led him to piles of what looked like stacked fruit. Some were the size of hydroponic watermelons, others no bigger than an orange.

Jake reached for one of the smaller ones, but Tani's sharp voice stopped him. "Be careful with those, unless you want to lose your arm!"

Jake jerked his hand back. Tani told him how the explosive was made from the distilled sap of a special tree and carefully poured into a hole cut in the end of each hollow gourd, which was sealed with wax.

A male native ran into the clearing, his eyes wide with fear. "The excavator monsters are approaching our village. We must stop them!"

Alarmed, the Citranese swiftly loaded sack after sack with their sap bombs, slung them with great care over their shoulders, and hurried into the woods. From the ease with which they all hefted the heavy-looking bombs and sacks, Jake realized their spindly arms and legs must be far stronger than he had thought.

Tani tugged at his hand and urged him to hurry after her. She led him to another area of the forest where the trees thinned and dapples of ruddy sunlight reached ground level. Tani pointed upward.

Jake looked, and at first he saw nothing unusual. Then he noticed hundreds of vines woven together into a huge netlike array that extended to the tops of the trees high above. Branches, palm leaves, and grasses were clumped together to form platforms. A metallic gleam made the tangled vines look like the tensile cables Jake had seen on Deep Space Nine. He reached up and grabbed one of the vines. It felt cold and hard, like metal.

"Did you build this?" Jake asked.

"They did," said Tani.

On the platforms high above sat a group of four-winged flying creatures. Their sleek, triangular heads caught the coppery sunlight, glinting on long, curved beaks. Their four wings—translucent like those of a dragonfly—beat slowly as they perched in their tree aeries. The splashing sunlight colored the wings with constantly changing patterns.

Tani signaled with her hand and held out her forearm. One of the creatures dropped beak-first from its platform, tucked in its wings, and streaked toward them. Alarmed, Jake wanted to dash into thicker woods, but since Tani didn't seem in the least alarmed, *he* certainly wasn't going to bolt.

Just before the large creature collided with them, it extended its wings, pulled up, and landed softly on Tani's arm. Its sleek, elongated body extended well above Tani's head. Its eyes were level with Jake's, and they regarded the boy with intelligence. Tani was signing with her free hand and appeared to be explaining something. The creature chirped once, and Tani stopped, satisfied.

"They help us fight the excavators," Tani told him.

"You've trained them to carry bombs!" Jake exclaimed. *Those* were the flying creatures he'd battled in the mothership's video games. He felt colder and colder inside with each new revelation. He had been so proud of himself for each successful hit, each target he defeated—but all along, the mining company had been deceiving him into attacking these living creatures!

"No one trains an Aarda," Tani said in a shocked voice. "We *asked* them if they would help us fight, and they agreed. All will die if our forests are destroyed."

The Aarda chirped, and Tani signed to it. The Aarda chirped again in a different key. "Kree wants you to stroke her," Tani informed Jake. Jake looked at the

needle-sharp talons and wicked beak, and wasn't sure he wanted to get near the creature. Tani urged, "Kree will consider it most impolite if you refuse her invitation."

Jake gulped and tentatively reached out his hand. The Aarda bent over and extended her head so that it was within reach. Jake rubbed the back of her neck and was surprised to touch smooth skin, rather than feathers, covering a layer of rock-hard muscle.

"It is time to meet your excavator monsters," Tani said angrily. "We have tried every defense, and still they come! Help us chase them away, Jake."

As he and Tani emerged from the forest under cloudy, leaden skies, Jake saw three automated excavators working their way methodically toward where they stood, and six more mining machines close behind. Above each excavator circled its flyer, buzzing like an angry hornet.

The excavators and their flying vanguards moved ever closer.

Desperately, Jake tried to think of a way to stop them.

On the mining ship, Dobb frowned at the empty seats at Jake and Nog's simulator console. *Where are they?* the Bajoran girl thought in annoyance.

They had not been late for their shift before. Perhaps Jake didn't think he could repeat his winning performance from yesterday, so he had been afraid to show up. Maybe he realized how hard a Bajoran could fight. He and Nog might even have decided to avoid her altogether by getting themselves assigned to another shift.

Well, that was not her problem. She still had a job to

do for the mining company. Dobb shook the distracting thoughts from her head, causing the silvery chains of her ear cuff to jangle.

She gripped her control stick and looked at the crude images on the colored screen in front of her. She concentrated on the geometric computer obstacles blocking the path of the excavator that her Benzite partner, Tandon, expertly maneuvered.

A pair of triangular needle-nosed blips darted down toward the excavator—enemy fighters—but she picked them off with a practiced ease that made her wish Jake and Nog were there to observe. Flying expert cover, she helped her partner avoid the tiny explosions. She could hear terse comments from other pairs around the room as they tallied damage or complained that the game this morning seemed more difficult than usual.

"Lightning storm brewing," Tandon warned, pointing at the eye-level readout. Dobb released her grip on the controls, rolled her shoulders, and stretched her hands, trying to relieve some of the tension that had built up since they started their shift.

She gripped the control stick again and fingered her weapons controls. "Okay," she said, with one last glance over at the empty position where Jake and Nog should have been. "Let's rack up some points."

Hardly daring to breathe, Nog stared through the ventilation grate into the ship's main control center. As he had hoped, Kwiltek sat there with a steaming cup, slurping tea through his beak and staring at the display monitors. Actual images of rich purple foliage and low huts lit by flashes of multicolored lightning played across the flickering screens.

The room was filled with guards now, though. One was even posted directly in front of the ventilator shaft. But they hadn't thought to check the grate in Nog's own chambers.

Fine, thought Nog, allowing himself a small smile of self-congratulation as he crept on down the air shaft. The extra guards here would make his job that much easier elsewhere.

The mothership's ventilation system was a maze of twists and turns, but Nog did not hesitate. Before long, he found himself at his destination. He pushed aside the metal screen covering the air duct and leaped to the floor—of Kwiltek's private quarters.

Aside from the main control center, this room held the only computer console that had access to all the mining station's systems. Nog knew this from the ship's layout schematics that he had studied. He sat down at Kwiltek's computer terminal and ran an admiring eye across its intricate controls.

Working quickly, he programmed an automatic message pod with a communication coded for his uncle Quark's eyes only, and sent it hurtling toward the Wormhole and Deep Space Nine. Then, pulling together every scrap of knowledge he had about computers, and relying more than a little bit on his Ferengi intuition, he began to hack into the video filters that supplied the game room.

As it began to rain, Jake helped several of the desperate natives wrestle wooden catapult frames into place just inside the forest. On each frame, the Citranese loaded a large watermelon-shaped gourd with a rag protruding from the back end. Homemade bombs.

Pairs of slender natives dispersed up and down the forest edge. One member of each pair carried a four-winged Aarda on his forearm, signing to the creature with his free hand as they got into attack position. Jake did his best to summarize the automated tactics the unwitting gamers on the mining ship were most likely to use against them.

The other Citranese partner carried sacks full of small gourds about the size of softballs. Still other villagers ran to the top of a nearby bluff, hundreds of meters above the approaching excavators.

It seemed the Citranese could offer only token resistance to the enormous machines grinding their way upslope. Jake bit his lip. *Think! Big as they are, excavators are only machines, and machines can be turned off or broken. They may have heavy armor, but they've got vulnerable parts, too.*

Jake studied the rolling factories as they drew closer. Their front panels opened, revealing black voids into which their lobster-claw scoops shoveled huge quantities of rock and dirt. *There must be conveyors inside those open mouths that transport the ore to the processing furnaces,* he thought. How could he knock out an internal smelter?

Every few minutes, black-brown slag spewed from the rear portion of each excavator in an ugly, clumped pile—waste rock left over after the furnaces extracted the latinum and other minerals. A turret swiveled back and forth on top of each mining machine, studded with disks of black glass—spectral sensors, constantly transmitting data from the surroundings.

Jake pointed, calling to the Citranese within earshot. "That's what we have to hit! If we shatter those sensors, the excavators will be blind!" Excited, the natives sent couriers to tell the other defenders.

The excavators approached the forest edge. The slender natives used torches to light the rags in the gourd-missiles. Seconds later, the gourds shot from the crude wooden catapults with bursts of fire and banshee screams, streaking toward the metal invaders.

Most of the bombs missed, fizzling out in the distance. But a few exploded into brilliant orange flames, rocking the huge excavators back on their treads and blasting large, discolored dents into their sides.

Still, the mining machines kept coming. Each time the Citranese launched a gourd, one of the attack flyers pulsed its phaser, trying to destroy the hidden catapult. But the Citranese quickly pulled their wooden launchers back into the shelter of the thick forest and to a new location.

Flying Aardas from the devastated slopes leaped into the air, clutching small explosive gourds in their talons. Their four wings hummed as they streaked in. Attack flyers fired phasers at them until the sky was full of the bright energy beams, like spears.

But the Aardas flew too fast for the eye to follow, diving and twisting and dodging the beams, weaving in and out only centimeters from searing death. The winged creatures were beautiful to watch as they worked their way closer and closer to their targets. Their swoops and lightning-swift changes of direction took Jake's breath away.

Once in position, the Aardas dived for the sensor turrets of the excavators as Jake had instructed, sleek purple blurs that left deafening sonic booms in their wake. The sound pounded Jake's eardrums.

The Aardas released their bombs as a team and pulled out of the dive. The gourds smashed into the machines and exploded into expanding fireballs that the swift Aardas barely outraced. With a pained shriek that tugged at Jake's heart, one Aarda spiraled to the ground, its wings burned by a phaser burst from a nearby flyer.

How can I protect these creatures? Jake wondered desperately. Then he remembered when he'd been piloting a flyer from his mothership console—when he *thought* he was just playing games—and he had zapped a river with his phaser to create a pillar of steam. The Aardas could pull the same trick with their bombs! Jake hurried over to a group of nearby Aarda handlers and told them his new plan.

Meanwhile, the little bangas, ignored by the mining company's flyers, bounced toward the excavators in a series of small hops, never leaping more than half a meter above the ground. Their dark fur blended well with the gouged dirt hillsides. Each living ball carried several orange gourds secured to its top, camouflaged with a piece of woven cloth.

A banga at Jake's feet buzzed in anxiety as one of its

companions got to within meters of an excavator's caterpillar tread. The banga deposited its bomb on the inside of the tread before hopping away.

As the caterpillar treads crushed the gourd, the home-made bomb exploded, blowing a section out of the tread and causing the excavator to twist to the right. The gathered Citranese sent up a cheer, and Tani rushed over to stroke the brave banga when it bounced back to pick up more gourds with its harness.

Then an Aarda slammed a gourd bomb directly onto the turret of another excavator, and a whole section of black sensor disks shattered in flame. The mining machine lurched to the side, then backed the other way. Blind, it slammed headlong into a neighboring machine. The excavator reminded Jake of a drunk Klingon he'd seen in Quark's bar, colliding with other patrons as he wove his way back to his table.

Another Aarda dive-bombed a gourd into one of the attack flyers circling the battlefield, skillfully dodging its phaser burst. The winged creature streaked away as a mushroom of flame and smoke erupted from the engine. But a nearby attack flyer, sensing the disturbance, hit the Aarda with a full phaser blast. Jake thought he heard a shriek from the Aarda before it turned into a blazing cinder.

The sky grew dark with smoke from burning equipment and exploding bombs. Two excavators now stood motionless, their turret sensors blown apart, while a third lay on its side, the victim of a well-aimed gourd. A fourth lurched in aimless circles, minus one complete caterpillar tread that the bangas' bombs had destroyed.

Boulders and tree trunks tumbled down the nearby bluff, dislodged by the Citranese on its summit. These battered the sides of the remaining excavators but did little damage.

Then Jake realized that more than battlefield smoke had turned the sky a deep gray-black. A thick mass of storm clouds had piled up, and he could feel the electrical tension in the air, so strong that the hairs on the back of his neck stood at attention.

The thunderstorm broke with a vengeance. Torrents of water poured from the sky, the rain heavy enough to obscure the details of the nearby excavators. He saw them only as immense dark shapes, blurry shadow creatures. The raw dirt quickly turned to ooze, and the machines floundered, sloshing and sliding, making little headway.

Jake watched as some of the automated flyers, unable to stay aloft in the gale-force winds, landed on the backs of the big excavators. The rain stung his cheeks, and his clammy clothes clung to his skin, but he barely noticed the discomfort. *Now's our chance to do something while those flyers are grounded,* Jake thought. *We must disable the remaining excavators.*

CHAPTER 10

In the simulation room, Dobb pinched herself. She must have been concentrating harder on the game than she had thought. Her eyes were beginning to play tricks on her.

For just a moment, the gaming screen before her had *changed,* fluttered. It had seemed as if she was looking at real trees rather than a crystal forest, delicate gossamer-winged creatures instead of imaginary needle-nosed fighters, flesh-and-blood natives instead of rocky obstacles.

Working the controls with one hand, Dobb rubbed at her eyes. When she looked up again, crude animated lightning flashed across the screen. The picture had returned to normal.

In confusion, Dobb rubbed her ridged nose. Colored lightning lit the screen again, and she flinched as a piercing howl sounded near her from another station.

"I'm hit! My sensors are disabled. Pull out, pull out!" She could hear panic in the voice of the bewildered excavator driver, followed by a grinding crash and a wail as the partner who had been flying cover also lost control of his machine. Groans and cries of outrage erupted around Dobb as other equipment failed or was destroyed.

Her own screen altered again, showing her the clear image of purplish trees against a stormy sky. Dobb used one sleeve to blot perspiration from her forehead and was relieved when the screen display returned to normal. She could hear the loud, raspy breathing of her Benzite partner and wondered if he had noticed her acting unusual.

"Incoming," Tandon snapped in a tight voice. "Above you and to the left."

Drawing in a deep breath, she took a firmer hold of the control stick. "I'm on them." She veered to intercept the needle-nosed fighters. The picture rippled and changed, still showing crude and flat crystals, but now they were lumpier and more purplish. Like trees.

The enemy flyers she was tracking were still fighters, but now they had iridescent gossamer wings. Dobb's heart raced. She hardly noticed the shouts and confusion of the others around her.

Focus, she told herself. She made a dive toward the enemy fighters, but they banked and swooped down in an evasive maneuver. She followed, readying her weapons as the fighters dipped close to a stream, skimming low. One of the fighters dropped a tiny bomb into the water in front of her. The explosion sent up a blinding cloud of steam, enveloping her craft.

Dobb pulled up sharply, rolled, and narrowly missed the top of a large crystal as she emerged from the vapor.

That was a close one, she thought, her pulse pounding in her ears. She hadn't expected something like that from the game—from Jake maybe, but . . .

Dobb's head reeled. She pushed back from the simulator console, trying to think. Something was very wrong here.

Rainbow-colored lightning bolts sizzled through the darkened sky, striking the hilltop and sending the Citranese natives scurrying downslope for safety.

Gazing at one of the mammoth machines fighting for purchase on the muddy hill, Jake envisioned its inside parts: conveyors and an ore smelter, containers to store refined metals, reactors to power the processes. But, most important, somewhere in the heart of all the hydraulics, gears, and circuit boards sat a computer that directed everything, taking commands transmitted from the mothership and converting them into actions—a computer, no doubt well shielded but without which the excavators could not operate.

And sensitive electronics, Jake knew, could be blown out and ruined by power surges—such as a discharge from an electrical storm.

"I've got an idea!" he shouted to nearby Tani, startling her. He ran around, gathering the natives, and called out his scheme, trying to make himself heard above the wind and thunder and the roar of struggling excavators.

The Citranese leader listened carefully, then whirled and began giving orders, waving his slender arms. All nearby Citranese, including Tani, ran into the forest. Some scurried up trees and slashed at the metallic vines that hung from the branches. Others waited below to catch and knot the vines together into long cables. Teams carried the cables and raced upslope to the top of the bluff.

Jake did everything he could to help, but he panted with exhaustion. He marveled at the strength and stamina of these spindly-looking people as they charged up the steep incline, never slowing until they gained its summit.

As the rain came down and lightning streaked above them, pairs of Citranese took the downslope ends of the knotted cables and hurried toward the excavator machines. Jake rushed after Tani to pick up one of the ends.

The muddy slopes were so steep and slippery that Jake slid more than he ran. Jake struggled to hold up his part of the vine cable and keep pace with the seemingly tireless Tani as she sloshed through ankle-deep mud toward the excavator. Its treads fought for traction, spewing gouts of slop behind it.

Automated flyers soared across the skies, continuing to shoot into the slashing downpour, targeting the natives with phaser blasts that sent geysers of hot mud flying into the air.

"Where do we tie this vine?" Tani yelled when they reached the side of the machine, staying low. In front of Jake, the machine's massive rear treads spun. He didn't dare risk coming too close to those. And the stream of mud hurled by the machine made approach from behind impossible. He had to come in from the front, where the wide-open mouth of the excavator waited.

From the bottom of the enormous maw, two hydraulic arms protruded, ending in scoops with jagged sides designed to rip into the ground and shovel great loads of ore back into the excavator. The mechanical arms flailed about, trying to find purchase on the muddy slope.

"If I can tie this cable around the base of one of those hydraulic arms, we'll be set," Jake shouted to Tani. "It's got to be attached securely."

Tani nodded. Trying to keep his balance in the muck and ready to duck if a metal scoop flailed in his direction, Jake inched toward the arm's base.

Then he slipped on a patch of mud slicker than bearing grease. Out of control, Jake slid down the remaining meters to the metal arm—just as the arm swept toward him. The scoop caught Jake in the stomach and knocked the wind out of him.

He doubled over and fell forward onto the long, segmented arm. His head and chest dangled over it. As if sensing his presence, the arm lurched, carrying Jake up toward the grinding maw. Inside the opening, he glimpsed a throat of conveyor belts waiting for him—and at its other end, a red-hot glow.

The ore-smelting furnace!

* * *

Nog hunched over the master data pad in Kwiltek's quarters, grunting and nodding as he disabled one video-enhancement filter after another. He was just reprogramming the final one when Kwiltek overrode the door lock and marched into his quarters.

Nog jumped to his feet and dived for the door, ducking around the startled alien. He pelted up the dim hallway. Kwiltek's footsteps thundered behind him, and he whistled for guards with a shrill, fluting sound.

Nog sped up, running in blind panic. His short legs pumped to keep him ahead. The sound of loud thudding from behind told him that more guards had joined the pursuit. Almost slipping as he rounded the final corner, Nog burst into the gaming control room.

Startled faces looked up from the simulator consoles. He saw Dobb from across the room pushing back in confusion from her control panels. Nog dashed to the center of the room and leaped onto one of the consoles.

"Listen to me!" he cried, pointing at the real pictures that now filled the video screens. "That is not a dead world. There are animals and people down there. My partner, Jake, is down there on the planet—"

Mutters and shouts of disbelief threatened to drown out his speech.

"It's true," Dobb's voice broke in. "No one but Jake could have pulled that steam maneuver I just saw on our simulator screens. That was no *game* we just played."

"No, it's not a game," Nog said. "It's business—very *big* business. The planet below us is rich in latinum, and Kwiltek's company doesn't care if he has to wipe out a whole living world to get it." He paused as a ripple of surprised murmurs spread through the room.

"Kwiltek is using this planet. And all of you!" Nog said, pointing around the room at the other gamers. "Kwiltek brought us here with lies. He is using us to destroy this world." As he spoke, Nog couldn't believe he was putting lives ahead of profit. But Jake was down there . . .

He pointed to Kwiltek, who, along with the guards, angrily shoved his way toward the center of the room where Nog stood. "Do you want to be responsible for killing an entire world?" Nog shouted quickly, knowing the guards were about to grab him. "Do you want to let the mining company use you?"

The angry cries of the betrayed gamers drowned out all further speech.

The excavator's mechanical arm tossed Jake toward the hot furnace, and he crashed onto the conveyor belt in the middle of a pile of squishy mud. He fought his way, sputtering and gasping, out of the ooze.

The moment he lifted his head, Jake felt a searing blast of heat on one side of his face. Turning, he saw the ore smelter approaching as the conveyor drew him forward. He also realized that he still held the end of the metallic vine cable.

Desperately, Jake scrambled back toward the outside, pulling himself along the cable. His feet pumped furiously in the slick mud. He fell, banging his elbow painfully on the conveyor, then struggled to his feet

again, vividly imagining what would happen to him if he was swept into the furnace.

Reaching the mouth of the excavator, he got a welcome blast of cool wind and rain on his face. Tani held the metallic vine, keeping tension on it so he could climb. Silently, Jake thanked her for her quick thinking and leaped free of the excavator mouth. This time, he managed to knot the cable end around the base of the metal arm and stumble away to safety.

Tani jerked sharply on the cable two times, signaling her fellow Citranese on the top of the bluff to tie it to the tallest tree. Then she and Jake ran from the excavator as fast as they could.

A massive thunderhead towered over the bluff. As Jake watched, a brilliant, jagged bolt of green lightning arced from cloud to hilltop.

The lavender tree on the summit burst into flames, and lightning raced down the vine cable to the excavator machine. For several seconds, a halo of crackling, spitting electrical discharge surrounded it. The strong scent of ozone, tinged with burning electrical insulation, tickled Jake's nostrils.

The excavator stopped short, its treads, metal arms, and turret now immobile and shivering with spasmodic convulsions. Black, noxious smoke poured out of its mouth as it sank into the mud, wheezing and deactivated.

Then Tani pointed in excitement. "Look at the other excavators!" Two of them had also been short-circuited by the lightning racing down other vine cables. The remaining machines had switched their engines into reverse and retreated from the scene of the battle. They slipped and slid down the muddy slopes, losing all the ground they had gained in the past hour.

The cheers of the Citranese rang out over the noise of the receding excavators. One after another, the slender humanoids rushed toward Jake to thank him. The bangas bounced up and down in apparent glee. Tani wrapped her thin, strong arms around him and hugged him. She squeezed so tightly that he thought his ribs would crack.

Then the rumble of the retreating excavators suddenly ceased. They had stopped in their tracks! Though seemingly undamaged, their engines, running lights, and all systems seemed to have switched off . . . as if the gamers above had shut them down. The attack flyers settled onto special platforms on the excavators, powering down their jets.

At that moment, Jake heard the familiar hum of a transporter beam about to whisk him away to another location. His skin tingled.

Finally! As the Citranese began fading out around him, Jake called, "As soon as I get back to Deep Space Nine, I'll send the Federation to protect this planet. I promise!"

The last thing he saw before they all disappeared was Tani looking at him, her big blue eyes wide with astonishment and appreciation. He tried to smile at her, but the transporter took him away.

CHAPTER II

Nog was waiting for Jake in the mothership's transporter room, grinning from ear to enormous ear.

"Nog! I was beginning to think you'd never beam me back up," Jake said, rubbing his hands down his muddy uniform. "What happened?" Every muscle in his body was still tensed and ready for action. After the dangers he had faced on the planet, he found his friend's sharp-toothed grin a bit irritating. "I almost got killed down th—"

"Tell me later," Nog said. "I've got something to show you. You'll never believe it!" He rushed Jake down the corridors to the gaming room, where an amazing scene was unfolding.

The gamers from every shift, all two hundred of them, had crowded into the simulation room, angry. Even so, Jake and Nog had never known the room to be as quiet as it was now. No phaser blasts issued from the simulation console speakers. No lights flashed. No chimes tinkled overhead as the computers tallied scores. All of the outraged players had switched off their terminals in protest.

A low-pitched, grumbling murmur rippled through the group as the young gamers converged on one corner of the large chamber. Kwiltek stood backed into the corner, head held high, an unreadable expression on his birdlike face. Only three of his guards, two Andorians and a Gorn, were anywhere in evidence. The outnumbered guards looked around with nervous uncertainty, afraid to start shooting.

Nog jumped onto a chair and addressed the group. "Now that my partner is safely back from the planet—" He pulled a dripping and muddy Jake up beside him, and the gamers cheered. "I think it's time we made a few things clear to the management of this mining station."

Jake cleared his throat and spoke in a loud voice. "What you're doing here is wrong, Kwiltek. People live on that planet, and that's *their* home you're destroying."

"We demand to be returned to our homes at once!" Dobb added.

"We won't do any more of your dirty work," another young humanoid said, crossing her arms over her chest. "You lied to us!"

"Yes, we are on strike!" Dobb's partner, Tandon, said, hissing through the wisps of vapor curling up from his respirator.

"Let's discuss this in a reasonable manner," Kwiltek warbled in a soothing tone. "You are mining company employees, after all. But I'm afraid that unless you agree

111

to sit down, stay calm, and renegotiate, I will have to suspend all payments of accrued wages until—"

Just then, the mothership's computer drowned out any further conversation with an emergency announcement: "Federation ship approaching at high speed! A Starfleet runabout requesting immediate docking. Mr. Kwiltek, your presence is required at once in the command center."

Grudgingly, the angry gamers let him out of his corner. "We want transport home, Kwiltek!" Dobb repeated, calling after him. Whistling in agitation, Kwiltek hurried toward a lift.

Nog stood on a chair so that everyone could see him despite his short stature. "Let's go greet our visitors!" he shouted, and he led his companions out of the simulator room. Jake followed, asking Nog who was on the approaching ship. But the Ferengi said only, "You'll see."

Just outside the mothership's main docking port, Nog and Jake squeezed into the reception area with as many other gamers as could fit. They heard the soft thunk of metal meeting metal; a slight shudder coursed through the floor under their feet. A moment after the hiss of equalizing pressures, a thick steel door rolled aside to reveal a fuming Commander Benjamin Sisko and an equally furious Rom and Quark.

"Dad!" Jake shouted, and he ran to his father. Nog was right behind him, hurrying over to his father and uncle, ducking low. Rom made a show of scolding his son, but both of the older Ferengi seemed secretly pleased.

Commander Sisko hugged his son hard, and Jake felt a tremendous relief that his father had arrived. "We got

Nog's emergency message pod and came right away," Sisko said, "but it looks as if you've managed to wrap up most of the trouble yourselves."

Just then, Kwiltek marched into the receiving area and confronted them. "Why have you come here? This is not Federation space. You have no jurisdiction over this planet."

"My nephew sent for me," Quark replied, stepping forward, "and rightly so. You have offended Ferengi honor. Perhaps you are not familiar with our Rules of Acquisition? My nephew has been trained in these principles since his youth. Nog, please familiarize Mr. Kwiltek with Rule Number 16."

Nog snapped to attention and recited with confidence: "A deal is a deal."

Quark shrugged eloquently. "It seems that you decided not to honor the business deal you made with my nephew and the human boy." The Ferengi's expression was almost apologetic, as if he had no choice in the matter.

"They're only children. They've lost nothing but a few days of their time," Kwiltek said. "Besides, why should your Ferengi customs matter to me?" he asked with an audible sneer.

Before Quark could answer, Sisko set Jake aside and glared over the heads of the other gamers at the birdlike alien. "Kwiltek!" he said in an icy, threatening tone.

Kwiltek flinched at the power of Sisko's voice. The commander of Deep Space Nine stalked forward to stand beside Quark, the veins on his neck standing out like indium tensocables. The mass of kids in front of him parted; no one wanted to get in *his* way.

Kwiltek straightened to his full height to face Sisko. "I cannot allow you to disrupt my mining operations in this manner. Please take your young and leave before I am forced to summon my station's guards."

"You mean the dozen guards we saw in *there*—with a couple of guys who looked like you?" Sisko asked, pointing toward the docking bay. "They climbed aboard a shuttle and left, towing a full ore hauler, just after we docked."

Kwiltek's face turned a strange shade of yellow-green.

Sisko nodded. "You have a lot of explaining to do, Mister," he said. "We have Starfleet reinforcements on the way—but perhaps we should see if we can work out a resolution before they get here?"

"A resolution?" Kwiltek said. "But we have done nothing to—"

The uproar of the betrayed gamers drowned out the rest of his words. Commander Sisko motioned for silence.

"You know it is forbidden to steal the resources of an inhabited planet," Sisko said. "The Federation takes its laws against strip-mining planets very seriously."

"But this planet is in the Gamma Quadrant, and therefore not under the jurisdiction of—" Kwiltek began indignantly.

"You are *licensed* through the United Federation of Planets," Sisko said, "and therefore bound by our laws. I have contacted the Federation Miners Guild and Trading Commission. If you refuse to comply with our laws, then your license will be revoked, and you will be unable to sell your ore anywhere in Federation space."

Kwiltek's face took on a shrewd look as Sisko began ticking his demands off on his fingers. "First, you must cease all operations on the planet below immediately."

Jake tugged on his father's elbow. "Uh, Dad, we already made a good start on that one."

Sisko laughed. "I'll bet you did." He turned back to Kwiltek and scowled. "Second, when the Starfleet ships arrive, I want you to arrange and pay for safe passage home for all of these young employees."

"And full wages! In latinum," Quark added. "As guaranteed in their contracts. Your mining company must pay in full—"

"But," Kwiltek interrupted, rubbing his horned claws together, "what if I am willing to give up my license? Your demands become meaningless."

Quark gave him a measuring look, bent his bald head toward Kwiltek's, and lowered his voice. "Maybe you're ignorant of Ferengi customs, but you must know our reputation as traders with many . . . connections?"

When Kwiltek whistled and nodded in acknowledgment, Quark continued. "If you do not honor your deal with my nephew and every one of these talented young people," he snapped, "you won't sell so much as a microgram of your ore through legal or *il*legal channels. Believe me. You won't be able to show your beak on the other side of the Wormhole without our knowing it."

Sisko nodded, then he sternly pointed a finger at Kwiltek again. "And to ensure that your company never

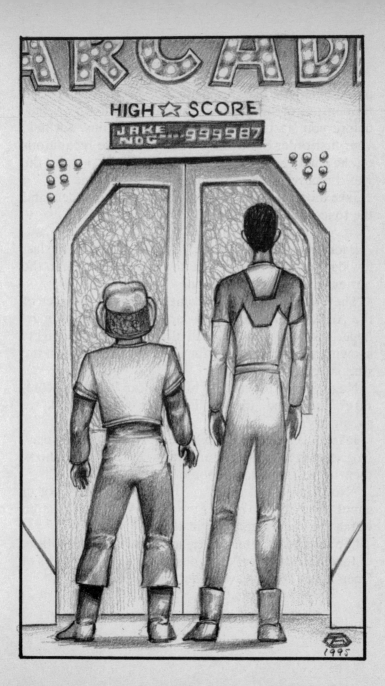

pulls something like this again, you will have a Federation inspector on your mothership at all times. But, before you start any new mining operations, Kwiltek, your first order of business will be to make reparations on the planet below, replanting their jungles, helping the world recover from the damage you have done."

Jake didn't need a Universal Translator to understand the tone of defeat in Kwiltek's wailing whistle.

Back on Deep Space Nine, Jake and Nog took the last few days of their school vacation to settle back into the normal routine of the station.

They walked along the Promenade to the entrance of the Arcade. Jake stopped to admire the glowing marquee, with their names still displayed in clear lights showing the highest score they had ever achieved in the simulator chamber.

Nog stood at his side. "Think we can beat that score, Jake?" he asked, his small eyes flashing. "Think we should try?"

Jake looked at him, then back up at the score display. Nog seemed nervous and uncertain. Both of them shook their heads at the same moment.

"No," Jake said, sighing. "I think I've had enough simulations to last me a *long* time. Why don't we go watch the ships coming in instead?"

"Sounds good to me," Nog agreed without hesitation.

Together, they went off to observe the docking ports of Deep Space Nine, leaving the Arcade behind.

About the Illustrator

TODD CAMERON HAMILTON is a self-taught art-
ist who has resided all his life in Chicago, Illinois. He
has been a professional illustrator for the past ten
years, specializing in fantasy, science fiction, and
horror. Todd is the current president of the Associa-
tion of Science Fiction and Fantasy Artists. His
original works grace many private and corporate
collections. He has co-authored two novels and several short stories. When he is not drawing, painting, or
writing, his interests include metalsmithing, puppet-
ry, and teaching.